COUNTESS DRACULA

COUNTESS DRACULA

BY

Carroll Borland

An Imprint of BearManor Media

Publisher
www.bearmanormedia.com
Production Manager
Christopher Mock
Editor in Chief
Philip J. Riley

BearManor Media
PO Box 71426
Albany, GA 31708

Second Edition - 2015
LCCN: 2015909515
ISBN: 1593938101

MagicImage wishes to thank the following individuals for their generous assistance:

Forrest J Ackerman
Rick Atkins
Buddy Barnett
Andy Hanson
Charles Heard
Marian L. Heard
Randy Krone
Lynn Naron
Anne Parten
Peter Mikkelsen

Gregory Wm. Mank - Author, actor, and teacher, has written the background material for MagicImage's Frankenstein and Mummy volumes. He is the author of *It's Alive! The Classic Cinema Saga of Frankenstein, The Hollywood Hissables, Karloff and Lugosi* and *Hollywood Cauldron*, as well as many features for such magazines as Films in Review, Cinefantastique, and Scarlet Street. Greg has received the Fanex Award for "Excellence in Genre Film Literature. He lives with his wife Barbara and children Jessica and Christopher in a hilltop home near Delta, PA, and is presently working on a book about Horror film heroines.

Anthony Brzezinski ~ (Front Cover Art) began selling art as a teenager and became a professional artist upon moving to Hollywood at age 20. His oil painting "The Voyeur" was sold to Columbia Studios as a prop for the Peter Fonda movie, "The Trip". Always involved with his friend and mentor Forrest J Ackerman, Brzezinski painted a Bela Lugosi cover from "Mark of the Vampire" for a Dutch magazine, "Horror". His work has appeared in numerous magazines, and was featured in a Washington D.C. show for the Federal Reserve System of the United States in 1987.

812-54

Carroll Borland 1935, photo by Jose Reyes

Within hours of sending this completed manuscript to the printing press, we heard the news that Carroll Borland Parten had made her final departure from this physical world. She pass away at 2:35 PM on Thursday, February 3rd, 1994, just 22 days shy of her 80th birthday. She had been ill with pneumonia, and had recently moved to Alexandria Virginia.

Charles Heard, her friend and number one supporter, tells us that she was very happy to see one of her lifetime dreams finally come true: the publication of her book, *Countess dracula.*

So sit back and enjoy this gift from a wonderful lady who made a lasting impact on the movies, and a positive impression on all those who came in contact with her.

Charles Heard with Carroll Borland, Los Angeles 1987

PREFACE

It's been a privilege, adventure, and high honor to have helped bring about the publication of Carroll Borland's novel, a veritable buried treasure created over six decades ago. *Countess Dracula* will prove to be a significant contribution to the ever-increasing wealth of Vampire literature. Written by the original "dark angel" of the vampire cinema, *Countess Dracula* has not been altered in any fashion since its completion in 1929. So here is a freshly-opened time capsule from that day replete with, as Carroll says, "punctures and all".

There has been evidence of an unseen presence working behind the scenes to bring this project together. Thanks also to Greg Mank, Forrest J Ackerman, Andy Hanson, Buddy Barnett, Anne Parten, Rick Atkins, Michael D. Stein, Chris Mock, Lynn Naron, Randy Krone, and Marian L. Heard.

Charles R. Heard
Dallas, Texas
August, 1993

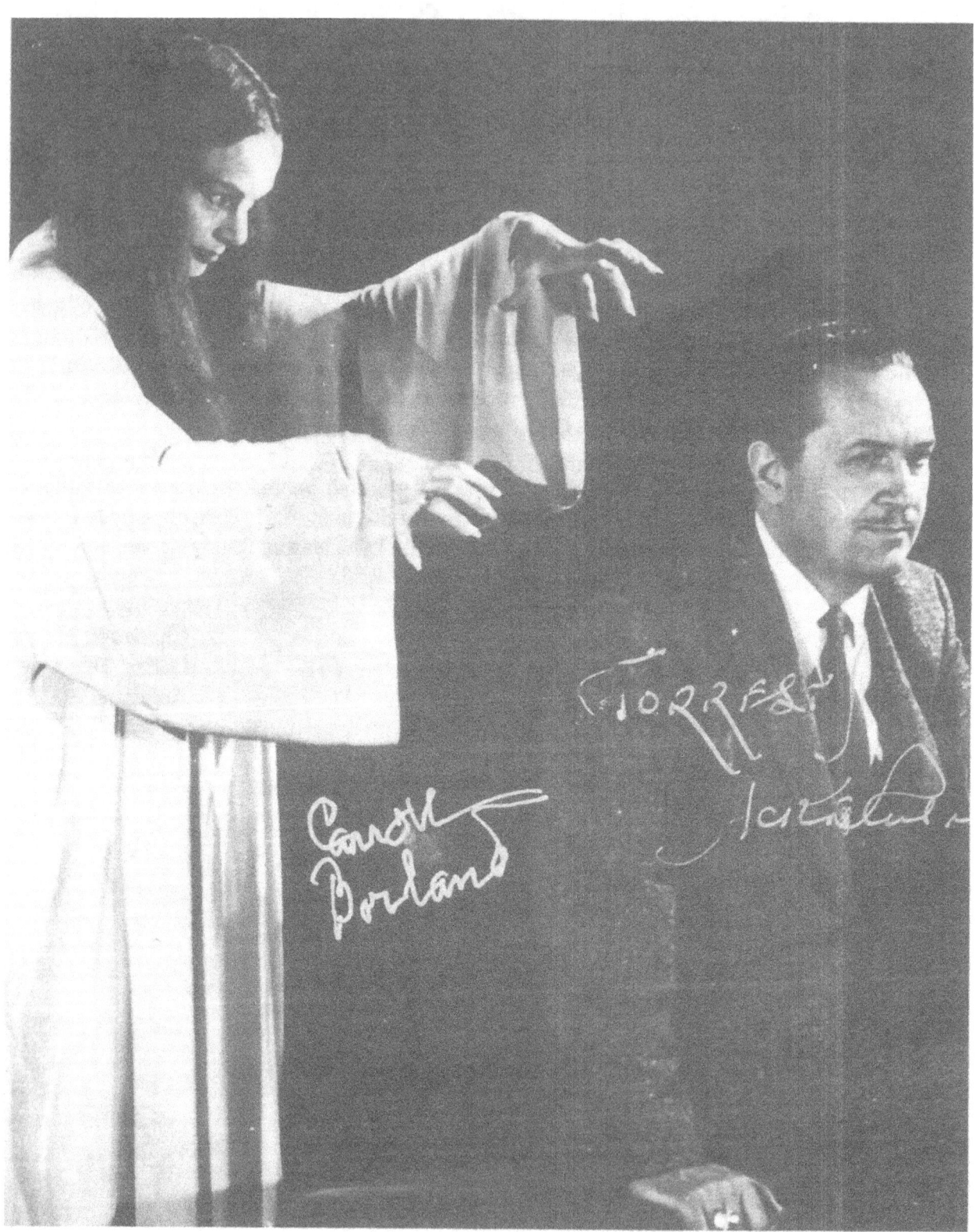

FORWARD

THE REEL DRACULA'S DAUGHTER
By
Forrest J Ackerman

A LOT OF BLOOD has flowed under the bridge since I was 18 and first saw Carroll Borland flap her wings (literally!) in *Mark of the Vampire*. I never dreamed that a quarter century later I would meet "Luna", be a guest in her home, interview her, be photographed with her by Walter J. Daugherty, famed "Photographer of the Mon-Stars"' write a famous feature about her in the pages of *Famous Monsters of Filmland*, "What Makes Luna-Tick?".

But all that fades like the sinking sun at twilight compared to the evening she spent in the original Ackermansion as she graced one of the 13 rooms - actually the dying, er, living room - as I joined a semicircle of her acolytes for an authorial reading of the manuscript you now hold in you hands in printed form. I seem to recall that among the packed audience (dinosaur animator David Allen had to stand outside by the open door) were Dr. Donald Reed, creator of the Count Dracula Society; Bill Warren, who would one day write the excellent imagi-movie volumes *Keep Watching the Skies!*; Donald F. Glut, who would author *The Dracula Book*; Wendayne *Rocket to the Rue Morgue* Ackerman; and numerous other individuals interested in vampires.

Here was this legendary woman, an actress who had been a protegee of Count Dracula himself and had known Bela Lugosi in his prime and her youth, reading aloud to us the story she had been inspired to write after seeing Bela in the 1928 stage version of *Dracula*. In its way it was almost like sitting at the feet of Mary Wollstonecraft Shelley and hearing her read *Frankenstein* for the first time!

So turn off the TV, turn down the lights so there's just enough illumination to read these pages, and across a gulf of more than half a century let Carroll Borland entertain you. Listen to her! - mistress of the night... what music she makes!

from the collection of Charles Heard

INTRODUCTION
By
Carroll Borland

Let me go back some sixty five years. I went to the Fulton Theater in Oakland with some high school friends to see *Dracula*, a play that presented a figure of my imagination... my dreams... my nightmares.

This tall, dark romantic figure walked out on the stage as the butler announced: "Count Dracula." I did not know it then, but my life changed in that moment as I, a late teenager, fell in love with Bela Lugosi. I had read the Bram Stoker book, practically memorizing it, so Lugosi presented a far different figure than the one that I had come to visualize from the pages of the book. Imagine if you will, this fascinating man, tall, dressed in evening clothes, the perfect teenaged girl's ideal... from his patent leather dark hair to his patent leather shoes. His mouth was curved and sardonic. His chin cleft and formidable. His eyes bluely fierce as an angry Siamese cat's and his voice like a seductive purr. On stage he was as seductive and threatening as a panther. This was a mesmeric man, drawing the sighs of the middle aged matrons of the audience, the embodiment of sexual appeal, a hypnotic demon-lover.

I went home from that theater in a daze; that night I lay awake and imagined... what if I were another woman? What if I were his love? What if... I could be with this magnetic creature with the hawklike profile?... Lugosi, Count Dracula. The next day I came home, went up to my dance studio in the marvelous Bernard Maybeck home where we lived in Oakland (yes, it is still there) and I started to write about my imagined meeting with him in *Countess Dracula*, my dream of the future. I soon realized that what I was doing was creating a history of someone else... Marise, a woman who was not I, but a modern lady who had met Count Dracula in the present. I had started to look up authorities of demonology... for example... the theory that he would return to life every fifty years or so to recruit more for his horde of vampires... why not Marise? How would they meet? How would he turn her into one of his own kind? After several months, as new ideas occurred, I would add them to my now nightly fantasies of this new, dreaded and attractive Dracula.

I can truthfully say, I think it is the only book which has logically, and using the facts as described in the Stoker work, explained Dracula's return. Some experts tell me that it is a true Gothic, and I am very proud of the adolescent who managed so well to get it down.

In 1929, Bela Lugosi returned to the Fulton Theatre once again. I wrote to him and told him that I had written a sequel to his play. He invited me and my mother to his hotel for breakfast and an interview. This was so like the middle-class continental gentleman he was.

Mr. Lugosi had long looked for another vehicle, something for a change, so he was intrigued by the idea of a new play and a refreshing concept of his character, as well as the addition of a female role to play with and against. He was interested in the *Countess* and my mother invited him to our house for breakfast so I could read it to him, for I surmise that he found English awkward to read. How well I remember him, cigar in hand and snapping his fingers for a cup of coffee as he stretched out on my grandfather's Biedermeir sofa, nodding or saying something about dialogue as I read it to him. He agreed to get in touch with Bram Stoker's estate to get permission to use the name Dracula for my heroine. Then, before I could rework the *Countess*, he went away and I went back to school. We corresponded sporadically after he left for Hollywood where Universal was filming *Dracula*. He often asked about "our book" and various persons tried to sell it.

One day I got a note from him in Los Angeles saying that the young lady who was playing Lucy in a stage version of *Dracula* was not working out. Could I come south and read for the part? I was on the next evening bus, yes, evening. In those days there were night buses, in which one slept in a bunk and arrived all set to cope with Los Angeles at dawn. I thought it delightful to lie, sleepless with excitement, gazing at slumbering cows in moon-washed meadows, thinking of all that I owed to that charming, demanding, arrogant, lovable man.

Of course, I got the part. Now, at 80 my next birthday, I realize that I never, in all my short acting career, read or auditioned for a part I did not get.

After playing Los Angeles, the tour continued and while appearing at the Lobero Theatre in Santa Barbara, Mr. Lugosi received a telegram calling him back to the studio. We all bade each other a fond farewell and *Countess Dracula* went back in my desk drawer. Years and years flowed on and *Countess* slept like her Lord in his coffin. I grew up, played Lugosi's daughter Luna in *Mark of the Vampire*, married John Ford's and Dietrich's publicist, lived in Europe for a time, and became a mother in 1952. Later I decided to go to Pacific Oaks College and learn something about Early Childhood. Eventually I became my second incarnation, Dr. Borland-Parten, instructor for UCLA in Human Development. Of course I did shows whenever I had the time; little and big theatres, radio, some movies.

Every once in a while *Countess Dracula* emerged. Agents said "but it is just more *Dracula*." Of course.

And then Charles Heard entered my life. First as a fan, then as a personal friend. Finally he said "Let's do something with *Countess Dracula* before she becomes a centenarian." So he did and I am sure that you wouldn't be holding this book in your hands today without my friend Charles. For him my heartfelt thanks.

Upon Bela Lugosi's death, I attended his funeral services but did not go to the cemetery. He is not there. Now, many years later, I know that he is happy that *Countess Dracula* is coming to light. He was always a good friend to me. I hope he will be to her too.

Carroll Borland
San Rafael, CA
July, 1993

Carroll Borland 1935

CARROLL BORLAND

by
Gregory Wm. Mank

When I first saw Bela Lugosi, he was playing a matinee of DRACULA in a theatre in Oakland. I'll never forget the moment he first stepped on to that stage - he was so wonderful, so magnificent. "This," I thought, "is the demon lover!"

- Carroll Borland

There are mists at night in the California valleys ...deep, swirling mists, drifting in like great, gray phantoms from the Pacific.

They swirl about a house in San Rafael, north of San Francisco, near the Napa Valley. There lives a retired actress and teacher. She has spent much of her life in Hollywood, where, almost 60 years ago, she created a hallmark role in the Cinema of Horror & Fantasy. Now, decades later, she's come home..." I, like an old salmon, have made my way upstream to the place where I was born to end my days..."

She has much in her life of which to be proud. She has been a devoted wife and mother. She had enjoyed a stage career which began when she won the California state-wide Shakespearean Actress Contest of 1931. She worked in Radio as both an actress and writer. And there was a sterling teaching career. Yet, always, there was a trademark of her creativity, her imagination, her theatrical passion.

It was the role of Luna, the climax of her life as protegee to the immortal "Count" himself - Bela Lugosi - in MGM's 1935 *Mark of the Vampire*.

Luna, the vampire girl, who flew on great bat wings...who hissed, just as Bram Stoker's vampire lady had hissed...who created the "look," the style and the sexuality for female vampires for generations to come.

It had been Bela Lugosi who had inspired her to write *Countess Dracula* over 60 years ago, after she saw him at an Oakland matinee of *Dracula* - and who had wanted *Countess Dracula* as a vehicle for himself.

It had been Lugosi who had invited Carroll to play Lucy to his *Dracula* onstage in a 1932 revival, and who delighted her with his sense of "devilish" humor - by dropping an ice cube down the back of her negligee at the Act II curtain.

It had been Lugosi who had walked hand-in-hand with her up and down Hollywood Boulevard, window-shopping, reciting from *Romeo and Juliet* (he in Hungarian, she in English) - and snarling when he saw a Christmas decoration featuring a portrait of his rival, Boris Karloff.

And it was Lugosi who had played Count Mora to her Luna in *Mark of the Vampire* - the vampire king who (in the film's original conception) had committed incest with his slinky daughter, and - in Gothic shame - strangled her to death and shot himself. They rose from their graves as vampires - a touch of sexual depravity that so embarrassed the film's director, the illustrious Tod Browning, that he omitted all references to it in the film's final release.

Bela Lugosi died in 1956, buried, as he had wished, in his Dracula cape - never living to see *Countess Dracula* published.

But now, almost 40 years after his death, almost 60 years after *Mark of the Vampire*, almost 65 years after Carroll wrote *Countess Dracula* and had read it to Bela as he ate doughnuts and sipped coffee on her family's couch, Bela Lugosi was back - so Carroll believed. He was there in the mist, the fog from the Pacific...still the demon lover he had immortalized on the stage and screen. And in the night, he spoke to the woman he had always called his "Little Carroll"...

"The book will be published...*Countess Dracula* will be published...OUR book will be published..."

For Carroll Borland, it was not a dream, or an hallucination. It was a promise being made by an actor Carroll had always loved, had always idolized as "the most wonderful man in the world."

The proof of the promise is in the hands of the reader.

Accompanying it is this too-brief biography of the extraordinary lady who wrote *Countess Dracula*.

****

I loved Bela dearly; he was a wonderful man - the most handsome, charming, delightful, delectable man in the whole wide world!

- Carroll Borland

17

Carroll Borland was born in Fresno February 25, 1914. Her parents (who were several generation Californians, of Scottish and Spanish descent) were in their 40s; when Carroll was born, it was feared she might not survive infancy. But survive she did - with an adventurous spirit and a touch of theatrical flair. At age 4, she began taking ballet lessons - "I had tiny ankles," says Carroll, "so my Mother thought it was a good idea." Her talent truly blossomed in high school, where Carroll won praise as a Shakespearean actress, playing Juliet, Rosalind, Cleopatra - and Lady Macbeth.

Carroll Borland at age 5, practicing ballet - San Francisco 1919

Then, one day in the late 1920s, she went to a theatre in Oakland, she went to see a matinee of *Dracula* - starring Bela Lugosi.

There was this tall, handsome, lanky Hungarian playing Dracula - with the most exciting blue eyes, like a Siamese cat. I came out of the play with my head in a whirl, having developed this adolescent crush on this beautiful man who, for me, WAS Dracula, the demon lover.

Bela Lugosi would stand onstage in Dracula, *in his cape, and scowl at the audience with those very blue eyes - and there wasn't a woman in the audience who didn't fall in love with him!*

Born Bela Blasko in Hungary on October 20, 1882, the 6'1" Lugosi (who took his stage name from his native village of Lugos) had enjoyed a glorious classical stage career in Europe - playing everyone from Romeo to Armand Duval to Jesus Christ; he had acted in European and American films; he had climaxed his career as *Dracula*, which had premiered on Broadway in October of 1927. A wounded War I veteran, a political exile from Hungary, Lugosi had found his destiny as *Dracula*.

There was an extra element in Carroll's attraction to the exotic, mysterious, but strangely familiar figure of Bela Lugosi.

I believe in Reincarnation. When Lugosi first made his entrance onstage in that matinee of Dracula, *I knew him from the moment I first saw him. I knew the man. I knew the spirit. In some other life, he had been my lover, or my mate. Later, I discovered that he felt the same way toward me.*

"The Demon Lover" - Exhibitor's Herald-World Nov. 15, 1930 - from the collection of Charles Heard

Carroll was fascinated. She ran to a "secondhand" store and bought a first edition of *Dracula*, shivering over Bram Stoker's 1897 Gothic classic. The Dracula figure haunted her young imagination; but not Stoker's aged, white-haired, fearsome figure, with scraggly moustache and red eyes. For Carroll, Dracula would always exist in the sleek, Valentino-form of Bela Lugosi.

"This was a man," laughs Carroll today, "I could really adore!"

Just as 18-year old Mary Shelley wrote Frankenstein, so did the 15-year old Carroll begin work on *Countess Dracula*. On Saturdays, after her ballet classes, Carroll would go to the dance studio, upstairs in her parent's home in Oakland, and compose *Countess Dracula* on her father's typewriter. She perpetuated the Dracula legend, advancing it 50 years, creating the character of Marisa, a "modern woman" of the 1930s who succumbed passionately to the immortal Count.

In 1929, the *Dracula* touring company played the Oakland area once more. Lugosi was still playing the Count - and Carroll contacted him about her book.

Bela liked the idea very much, and later called me and asked me to come down to the hotel and have breakfast with him. But, being the European gentleman he was, he of course invited my mother - he would never have considered asking me to come down alone!

Later, he would come out to our house, on Park Boulevard in Oakland, and I read him Countess Dracula. *He was very interested in it, but I had to read it to him. He could follow spoken English, but English is a funny language - it isn't always pronounced the way it looks. So I would read to him, and he would lie back on his sofa, smoke his cigars - those never-ending cigars! - and snap his fingers and point for coffee! Domineering - oh, I should say so! He wasn't used to American women. I thought it was very rude of him - but I got him the coffee!*

He liked to be read to; he liked this domestic thing. And of course, this is terrible, because it isn't appropriate for the terrible Dracula to lie around someone's house, enjoying coffee and donuts! But he was a very simple person that way...

She became Lugosi's "Little Carroll," a very special and dear friend; he became not only her friend, but

epitomized for Carroll her deepest beliefs and fascinations with the Theatre:

Pan is basically the God of the Theatre. I belong to Pan, and I love that Pan is the God of make-believe; if we love make-believe, we love Pan. Pan is a mystic personage. If you are alone in the forest, he whispers to you - a form of panic - but he is wonderful at the same time. Don't turn around!

Lugosi is "Pannish" and synonymous with the demon-lover. Pan is of the earth. I love him!

Lugosi was enthusiastic about *Countess Dracula*, as a book and a possible theatrical project for himself. He even personally contacted the Stoker estate to try to arrange the title clearance. But there were delays, and priorities, and the book's publication never came to pass. Bela's acting commitments and Carroll's studies separated the two unique friends - but not before a very memorable night for Carroll:

I kissed Bela, only once. It was one night, under the Magnolia tree, in front of my parents' house in Oakland. He said, he'd had such a good time; I said, "Oh, I've had such a wonderful time" - and he leaned over and he kissed me. To this day, I remember his Cupid's bow of a mouth - the most magnificent moment of my life.

I must add that Bela would have never thought of taking advantage of me. If he DID think it, he never did.

1931 was a major year for both Bela Lugosi and Carroll Borland. In February, Universal released the film of *Dracula*, with Lugosi recreating his stage role of the Count under Tod Browning's direction. It was the studio's top money-maker of the season, and Lugosi's performance became Hollywood folklore. Carroll, meanwhile, won a California statewide contest as Outstanding Young Shakespearean Actress - and a scholarship to University of California at Berkeley. Carroll followed her friend's Hollywood stardom.

However, neither stardom as *Dracula*, follow-up melodramas as *Murders in the Rue Morgue* (Universal, 1932) and *White Zombie* (United Artists, 1932), nor fan mail reportedly as voluminous as Gable's ("98% of it from women," Bela informed the press), could control Lugosi's reckless spending. In October of 1932, the movie star filed bankruptcy - listing his assets as $500 equity in furniture, and four suits. Although there was movie work, Lugosi felt he should return to the stage in a condensed version of *Dracula*.

And Carroll received a letter:

November 16, 1932

Dear Carroll; -

I am at present rehearsing a condensed version of the stage play Dracula *for a tour over the vaudeville circuit.*

The present LUCY, is not quite satisfactory, so if you were in a position to come down and take a chance, (At your own expense) I would arrange to have a reading of the part for you and if you CLICKED from the producer's standpoint, it would mean a possible long tour in a very good part.

With kindest personal regards always, I beg to be,

Sincerely,

Bela Lugosi

20

Carroll took a night bus from San Francisco to Hollywood - and won the part.

In rehearsals, Carroll had the opportunity to observe Lugosi "in action:"

Bela had an incredibly wonderful devilishness - that devilish charm! I have never known a man who could sit still in a room, and all the women were just drawn to him like pieces of iron to a magnet. He was incredible - the sexiest man I ever knew!

Carroll always has insisted that her relationship with Lugosi was platonic. However, that didn't prevent the friendship from having its own very special level of passion:

Playing Lucy with him, I had grown up in his eyes. I called him by his first name then. We would walk up and down Hollywood Boulevard after rehearsal, hand in hand, looking in the shop windows.

We would go to the Roosevelt Hotel, and have supper, and dance; I was a professional dancer, and he liked someone who could do a Viennese waltz. We would dance together, and I always remember being close to him while he was humming, dancing, that reverberation in his voice and chest...

Oh, we had such fun! We would play Shakespeare together - he in Hungarian, and I in English! We had a marvelous time - although we were speaking different languages, we each knew what the other was saying!

We had a beautiful time together. We were both young, somehow...

Bela presented a very cavalier, "I am never hurt" attitude to Carroll. He never spoke of his three failed marriages; he never mentioned his famous affair with Clara Bow; he never talked of the career mistakes which already were plaguing him (such as his having scorned the Monster role in *Frankenstein* - and having created his own "monster," Boris Karloff). However, one night, during the Christmas season, Bela revealed a flicker of the sensitivity which later dominated his terribly tragic life:

We were walking down Hollywood Boulevard, and in those days, the celebration for Christmas meant that every street light was decorated with a circle of lights,

and tinsel, with a star's picture inside.

It was after Frankenstein *had been released. Lugosi looked up - and there, in a circle of lights, was a picture of Boris Karloff.*

And I'll never forget Lugosi, looking up at that picture of Karloff, glaring at it, taking his cigar from his mouth. I'll never forget the look on his face. And I'll never forget the sound he made....

"Grrr..arrgh!"

I don't know whether it was Hungarian swear words, or just a growl! But we kept walking, and soon, he saw a picture of himself. "Ah!", shouted Bela - and he was happy again.

The *Dracula* tour would prove to be brief - but for Carroll, it is unforgettable:

Bela had sort of a childish sense of humor. Once when we were playing Dracula, *he had a drink backstage. And in the horrible clutching scene of Lucy fainting over his arm with the cape around her, a cube of ice went down my neck!*

To me, Bela was a charming, wonderful person but it was rather like having a large, tame panther around the house. A friendly panther. You can pull his whiskers - but you had to be very careful not to upset the panther. ...

Always, he treated me as a friendly playmate. It was wonderful.

The company got as far as Santa Barbara, and the tour disbanded. Carroll went back to Berkeley. Bela got married. On January 31, 1933, he eloped to Las Vegas with his 4th wife, 21-year old Lillian Arch, of Hungarian descent. Bela had been courting off-and-on for several years. The marriage would last 20 years (in 1938, Bela Lugosi Jr. would be born). Bela settled into happy married life. Carroll trained in Speech and Theatre at Berkeley, meanwhile joining the Columbia Broadcasting System as a staff actress. They lost touch, except for an occasional letter or Christmas greeting.

Then - come the Holiday Season of 1934 - Fate brought Bela Lugosi and Carroll Borland back together again.

****

A Beauty From
Out Of the Shadow
Of Doom. The
Cruelest Woman
In Two Worlds!

- Carroll Borland's publicity from
Mark of the Vampire

Indeed, it sounded like the Horror Movie to end all Horror Movies.

The studio was Metro-Goldwyn-Mayer, where there were "More stars than there were in the Heavens" - Garbo, Gable, Harlow, Crawford, MacDonald & Eddy, Laurel & Hardy.

The director was Tod Browning - the "Edgar Allan Poe of the Screen," director of such Lon Chaney Silents as *The Unholy Three* (1925), *London after Midnight* (1927) and *West of Zanzibar* (1928), and of Universal's *Dracula* starring Lugosi. Indeed, the new project was a combination of Browning's *London after Midnight* and *Dracula* a horror tale tentatively titled *Vampires of Prague*.

And the actor signed to play the vampire, "Count Mora" was Bela Lugosi.

Chaney Sr. in *London after Midnight* had played both professor and vampire; *Vampires of Prague* divided the roles, presenting "Professor Zelen" to the studio's venerable character star, Oscar-winner Lionel Barrymore; Lugosi naturally took the vampire part. Lionel Atwill, star of such melodramas as 1932's *Doctor X* and 1933's *The Vampire Bat* and *Mystery of the Wax Museum*, was cast as the Inspector. And the leading lady was Elizabeth Allan, who had just scored as the frail, doomed mother of *David Copperfield*.

However, yet-to-be-cast was the role of "Luna," vampire daughter of Count Mora. Edna Tichenor had played the part in *London after Midnight*; in his original scenario Guy (*Werewolf of Paris*) Endore had created a chilling folklore for Count Mora and Luna: They had committed incest, after which the Count strangled his daughter, and shot himself. They arose as vampires.

MGM began a publicity-crazy search for a Luna - later claiming in the pressbook that the studio had received 32 pounds of photographs from actresses aspiring to play Luna.

And Carroll Borland learned about it.

Carroll felt this was her destiny. She left Berkeley, and came to Hollywood, determined to win this role and create a performance on film, with Bela Lugosi, that would last for generations to come.

Naturally, arriving in the movie capital, Carroll contacted Bela Lugosi. In 1935, Bela lived in Movie Star fashion at 2835 Westshire Drive - a 3-story, red-brick castle, atop a hill and at the edge of cliff in the Hollywood Hills, not far from the *Hollywoodland* sign. There Bela enjoyed his cigars, his Dobermans, his sociology books and stamp collection, and the parties he and Lillian hosted, where Gypsy musicians played until dawn. Yet, for all his fame and glory, Bela - learning of Carroll's wish to play in *Mark of the Vampire* - advised her NOT to try out for the part.

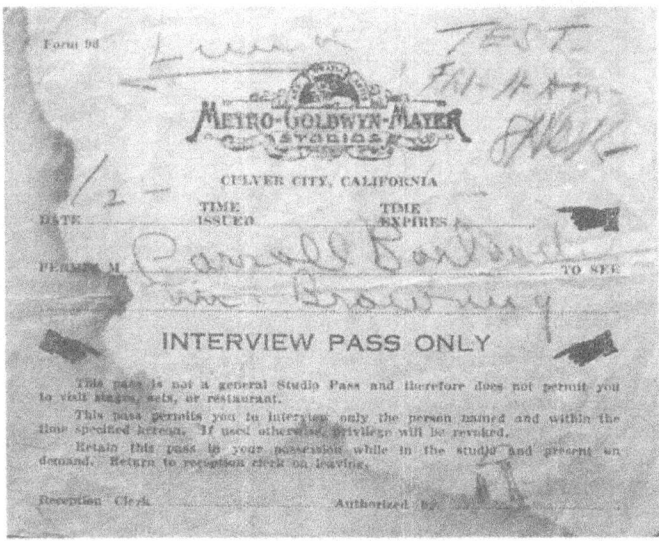

Luna test - January 2, 1935

"If you do this," warned Bela ominously, "you will be stuck haunting houses - as I have been!"

Carroll could not be dissuaded, so Bela became her ally. She acquired an agent, and got a test at MGM - where Browning decreed she was "too short" to play opposite the towering Lugosi. Then Bela announced he wanted to test with her - pretending he didn't know Carroll at all. He reported for the test with his cape ("I never play the vampire without my cape!" he claimed), and scrunched down to look less tall. Carroll, meanwhile, wore her high heels.

"They were amazed that I had all of Lugosi's gestures and personality!" recalls Carroll.

However, even having Bela Lugosi as an ally was not power enough to storm the fortress that was MGM in 1935. Although she would be touted as Tod Browning's "discovery," Browning actually had no opinion as to the casting of this rich role. So *Vampires of Prague*'s assistant director made Carroll an offer: $150 paid to him, under the table, and the role of Luna would be hers.

"Standard procedure, in those days," recalls Carroll - and a lot more honorable than the style in which some young actresses managed to get their big break. Carroll realized this role was her Fate, so her agent

paid the assistant director the $150.

"That's how I got the role," says Carroll. "I bought it."

Vampires of Prague now had its "Luna," and MGM began publicizing Carroll as "Cinderella in a Nightmare".

The "political" situation of *Vampires of Prague* was curious. Tod Browning, long with MGM, was out-of-favor, having directed the disastrous *Freaks* of 1932. For Browning's new film, MGM slapped him with a budget of only $208,734.01 - chicken feed for an MGM film. Also, Browning had a history of alcohol problems, and Eddie Mannix - L. B. Mayer's trouble shooter and studio manager - produced *Vampires of Prague* personally, presumably to keep an eye on Browning.

The "Luna look" that defined the female vampire in cinema for the next half century

None of these problems affected Carroll. She had won the coveted role, and now joyously reported to makeup at MGM to create the "Luna" look:

'IS BEAUTY REALLY ONLY SKIN DEEP?'

Hollywood's make-up men contend it is, adding by way of gratuitous pun, "The 'eyes' have 'it'." At all events they have proved the point with **Carrol Borland**. Ordinarily it is Hollywood's chore to transform plain girls into beauties. In this instance the trick was done in reverse. The pictures show the metamorphosis of Miss Borland, beginning as a collegiate sub-deb, going to her first test for "Vampires of Prague" and concluding as she will be on the screen as the "un-dead daughter" of the picture's arch-villain.

Oakland Trib

Exclusive Associated Press Service
United Press Associations

OAKLAND, CALIF., TUESDAY, MARCH 12, 19

U. C. Girl Becomes Screen Siren; Eyes Give Her Role

The graduation of Myrna Loy from the slinky Oriental roles in which she attained film distinction to the sophisticated American girl types she has been portraying in recent releases has made way for the introduction of another University of California girl to Hollywood.

Curiously, Metro-Goldwyn-Mayer, the studio which took the freckled Montana youngster, Miss Loy, and converted her into a slant-eyed siren, is now faced with the task of converting Carroll Borland, daughter of Mr. and Mrs. Guy H. Borland of 2319 Park Boulevard into a vampire.

In both cases the make-up department is starting with the eyes. Unlike in type the Misses Loy and Borland have eyes that are so shaped that make-up can develop character from them. The rest will be up to the actress and her director, Tod Browning.

It was Browning who first discerned the signs of promise in Miss Borland. Unable to find a suitable type for the siren in "Vampires of Prague" he petitioned the casting offices and agents for types. Miss Borland. Unable to find a suitable photographs to an agent and was chosen without delay.

Previously her experience had been on the stage of Wheeler Hall at the University of California and, briefly, in dramatic stock at the Roosevelt Theater in Oakland. Eva Le Gallienne offered her a place in her Civic Repertory in New York but Miss Borland was unable to make the trip East.

"Vampires of Prague" is now in production with Miss Borland playing the "un-dead daughter" of Bela Lugosi. Meantime she is making tests for the role of the second wife in "Good Earth" which is now being cast.

24

Naturally, I reported to Women's Makeup at MGM. Well, they said they couldn't do anything with my face - and sent me to the MEN'S makeup department!

There was a young makeup apprentice there at the time - his name was Bill Tuttle. They were going to cut and curl my hair, and I kept saying "No!"; eventually, we worked out that adaptation of Lugosi's Dracula face, which was very much like mine anyway. Finally, one day, I was sitting there, brushing my long straight hair, trying to decide what to do with it...

Suddenly, Bill Tuttle said - "That's it! Part it in the middle, and leave it down, on either side of your face!"

Well, now that face is the classic vampire face, with the hair parted that way. Tuttle was willing to take a chance, and I didn't have to be pretty - just be me, with my face - and my big mouth the way it was! Today, Bill Tuttle is probably the major Makeup Man in Hollywood, and "Luna" was one of his first attempts, and we did it together - as kids.

I still laugh, though, when I remember being sent to the MEN'S Makeup department. Every morning I would go in there, and Nelson Eddy was there, preparing for Naughty Marietta. *And Nelson and I would sit there and SING every morning in the Men's Makeup department!*

```
                   1/26/35

Pinky Tomlin.................10:30

Miss Allen..................9:00
Mr. Barrymore...............9:00
Mr. Atwill..................9:30
Mr. Lugosi..................6:30 p.m.
Miss Borland................6:30

Mr. Eddy....................11:00
Miss McDonald...............9:00
```

*Shooting schedule at MGM
from Carroll Borland's scrapbook*

Mark of the Vampire (still titled *Vampires of Prague*) began shooting Saturday, January 12, 1935 - 10 days after James Whale began directing Karloff in *Bride of Frankenstein* at Universal City. In her Luna makeup and shroud ("By Adrian!" Carroll laughs), the novice actress arrived on the soundstage - and met her venerable co-stars, whom MGM would publicize as "The Screen's Greatest Cast of Mystifiers":

Carroll in publicity photo with Lionel Barrymore - background

It was fun being around Lionel Barrymore. He was always kind to me, and would pat me on the head. Unfortunately, he was suffering greatly at the time - troubled with arthritis. He had been an excellent etcher, and now his fingers were just freezing into those lumpy fingers that wouldn't work anymore. Before long, he'd be in a wheelchair, in which he acted for most of the rest of his career.

Lionel Atwill - oh, wasn't he fun! Such fun! He was rather stern, very British, sort of the bumbling Col. Blimp in personality - and awfully opinionated! But he was right, so he had a RIGHT to be!

Very soon, all of us - Barrymore, Atwill, Jean Hersholt, Holmes Herbert, and, of course, Lugosi - we formed a little intellectual club. I was reading Ludwig's Napoleon *at the time, and these were European gentlemen, most of them, brought up on Napoleonic history. So we would have wonderful talks and arguments, and had our own little clique. It was fun, because they didn't treat me as an impertinent young female. I was a part of this group that was discussing things.*

It was a marvelous situation! And I learned a lot from them!

MGM was rip-roaring with activity at this time: Jean Harlow was starring in *Reckless*, Jeanette MacDonald and Nelson Eddy warbling in *Naughty Marietta*, Paul Lukas smoothly starring in *The Casino Murder Case*, Pinkie Tomlin starring in *Times Square Lady*, and Una Merkel and Charles Butterworth top-lining *Public Enemy No. 2*. It was a thrill for Carroll, and every day was a new and glamorous adventure as she beheld the legendary MGM stars on the lot and in the commissary.

However, come lunch, it became harder for her to star-gaze than she had wished "There was a rather disturbing persona that Bela and I presented," says Carroll.

I used to go to the cafeteria on the lot at MGM to eat lunch, and I got very good treatment - escorted into a little back room. Then I realized I got this treatment because people did not want to sit and look at me while they were eating! The people had complained - they thought I was wearing such a horrible makeup! It hadn't occurred to me that it was anything but plain, good old Dracula makeup.

Bela didn't accompany me - he went off with other friends; I usually ate by myself, or with Guy Endore and his wife, Henrietta. I became very good friends with the Endores; they had a small child, and lived in an apartment close to where I lived. We would sometimes spend evenings together, talking about demonology and witchcraft, and Guy's work, and how Henrietta had worked in Macy's basement (I think) while Guy was writing Werewolf of Paris. *They were very young at the time, and it was fun being with people of my own age.*

Indeed, there was a difference, Carroll noticed, in how Bela treated her on the *Mark of the Vampire* set. Once Carroll's "friendly panther," he was now her Dutch uncle - a married, domesticated male who kept his life with Lillian apart from his former protegee. Yet, in his new, avuncular way, he still doted on her - and treated her with affection and love.

Bela would say, "Pull your skirts down," "Keep your feet together," "Don't say 'Damn'" - that sort of thing. He wanted me to be a VERY good girl! But, above everything else, Bela had one special commandment for me: "Don't associate with Elizabeth Allan, because she has a bad reputation!"

Yes, I remember well the gossip on the set - for Elizabeth Allan supposedly was having an affair with Mark of the Vampire's producer, Eddie Mannix. "That's why she is here now!" Bela would hiss to me on the set. "So you stay over here with us" - and he'd direct me back to our little clique!

"Luna" ,Carroll Borland, puts "Irena", Elizabeth Allan, in a trance before biting her on the neck in Mark of the Vampire.

It was all part of Bela's new protective role, which he played with a passion.*

Bela, every day, saw to it that Carroll got home safely. Each evening, Lillian ("a dear person," says Carroll) would pick up Bela at the MGM lot (he never learned to drive). "We would laugh in the car about my adolescent crush on Bela," says Carroll. "Of course, I STILL adored him - and still do!" Bela made sure they drove Carroll home to her apartment at Franklin Avenue and Wilcox Avenue, above Hollywood Boulevard, before they went home to their castle above Beachwood Drive.

We would be tired at the end of the day; I had my hair glued to the side of my face with spirit gum, and Lugosi had this bullet wound stuck on him, and we would just pile into the car and go home. Well, it was so funny! This truck pulled up. I was sitting on the right hand side in the back seat; and Lugosi never drove, so he, too, was on the right hand side in the front seat as Lillian drove.

This truck with a cart of chickens on it, pulled up next to us.

Well, the truck driver looked first at Lugosi with this bullet wound in his head, and then at "Luna" in the back seat, did the most perfect double take I've ever seen, then his foot must have slipped - and the truck shot right up onto the sidewalk, into someone's front yard, the chickens screaming their heads off!

And Lugosi said - "Why did he do that?"

I was laughing so hard, I couldn't stand it! If it had been staged, you'd have said, "That's just slapstick comedy" - but it really happened!

Bela displayed his own humor, too, as Carroll laughs:

---

* As for Miss Allan and Mr. Mannix...Elizabeth Allan would later be blackballed out of Hollywood, after she sued Louis B. Mayer for casting Rosalind Russell in *The Citadel* - a role Mayer allegedly had promised Miss Allan. She died in 1990. As for Eddie Mannix, he died in 1963, and there are rumors today that he killed George "Superman" Reeves, whose 1959 death was considered officially suicide, because of Reeves' relationship with Mannix's wife.

Bela had a nice sense of humor. I remember once, on the Mark of the Vampire *set, we waited all day as they put up a door we had to go through - I don't know what held it up. After about two hours of sitting there, I said, "What do you think they're doing?" And Bela sad, "Carroll, I think they're AGING the door!"*

Soon, on *Mark of the Vampire*, the day came to shoot Carroll's favorite vignette from *Mark of the Vampire* - Luna's flying sequence in Borotyn Castle:

For me, the main moment in Mark of the Vampire *was the flying scene. I love it! It happens so fast that if you drop your handkerchief and pick it up, it's over - but still, that's what people remember.*

Of course, that wasn't trick photography - I was literally "flying!"

First of all, MGM hired a jockey as a stand-in for me; to fix the lights exactly, someone had to be up there. It was about the height of a telephone pole, and they put him up there, in the special flying harness I eventually wore, and the great bat wings and all.

Well, the man got airsick - he couldn't stand it - so I took over!

So, they hung me up there, and let me dangle, until they focused everything properly. The jockey didn't like being up that high, but I thought it was a terribly exciting thing to do - it was fun! The soundstage had just been used in Naughty Marietta, *for a scene where Jeanette MacDonald released birds - and some of the birds were still up there, with me!*

As for the landing - that really was funny. The men who were landing me - one on the body part, and the other on the "tail," so to speak - didn't have sense enough to realize that my feet had to come down first. So, the two would land me together - and they'd land me right on my belly, and I'd go skidding across the canvas. VERY uncomfortable. Finally, they got the idea that even BATS land feet first, I guess!

All through the shooting, Carroll was surprised by the laid-back manner of Tod Browning. "The Edgar Allan Poe of the Screen" arrived each day in sporty vests ("Plaids and tweeds," remembers Carroll), flopped into his director's chair, and mumbled the simplest of traffic directions to Carroll and her co-players. Come the climax of *Mark of the Vampire*, where Luna "attacks" Irena, Carroll and the redoubtable Browning had a "showdown" of sorts - with classic consequences:

Tod Browning was an amazing man as a Director. Everybody asks what it was like working with him, and I must say, "I don't know - he just turned me loose."

In the book Dracula, *it says that Lucy turned around, and her face looked like a Japanese mask - the square mouth, the horror mask - and she hissed like an angry cat.*

Well, in this scene, where I'm surprised while biting Elizabeth Allan on the neck, Browning said, "I want you to turn around, snarl like a wolf and growl." Who am I to tell Tod Browning how it should be? But I was 20 years old, and would have told anybody anything!

So I said, "Oh no - that's not the way it is at all! I quoted the book, about the square mouth, and I hissed.

And Tod Browning said, "I like that - try it!" So I did - he said "That works" - and so they kept it.

Well, I've been so amused. When Bob Bloch wrote The House That Dripped Blood, *he had a vampire coming up out of her coffin, and she turned around and hissed that way. The next time I saw Bob at the Count Dracula Society, I said, "Thank you for doing that!" And Bob said, "I'm glad you noticed. I did it for you - because that's RIGHT." Now, I see it all the time - anytime you see a vampire in one of those films, they turn around and hiss.*

And I say, "Aha! That's my contribution to the Art of the Cinema!"

In Carroll's opinion, the true dynamo of *Mark of the Vampire* was not Tod Browning, but the cinematographer, James Wong Howe. "He really was a genius," says Carroll. "We were both young San Franciscans, and would talk about who and what we remembered from our home town. He really was wonderful - an incredible person." Howe would win 16 Academy nominations for his cinematography, and two Oscars - for *The Rose Tattoo* (1955) and *Hud* (1963).

Vampires of Prague - soon officially retitled *Mark of the Vampire* - crept to completion. There were problems. Elizabeth Allan protested that James Wong Howe was spending too much time bringing out the best in Bela and Carroll, and not devoting enough expertise to showcasing Elizabeth's own glamour.

Then there was the ending.

"We had BELIEVED in it!" says Carroll today, still unhappy about the finale which presented the vampires as mere actors, trying to scare a confession out of

A rare behind-the-scenes shot taken during the filming of Mark of the Vampire

the true murderer, Jean Hersholt. Browning had kept the tag a secret until well into production; while it might have worked in *London after Midnight*, Bela, Carroll and most of the cast thought it a cop-out.

Carroll made a suggestion: why not have a telegram arrive - from the actors, apologizing for not having arrived in time? True vampires after all! But Tod Browning would have none of it, and *Mark of the Vampire* would retain its controversial finale:

LUGOSI: This vampire business - it has given me a great idea for a new act. Luna, in the new act, I will be the vampire. Did you watch me? I gave ALL of me! I was greater than any REAL vampire!

CARROLL: Sure, sure, but get off your makeup!

"That stupid ending!" says Carroll. "How can one possibly say, 'Oh, so it was only a troupe of acrobats and actors?' Oh, come now!"

Mark of the Vampire finally "wrapped" February 20, 1935 - 10 days over the original schedule; the final cost would be $305,177.90 - almost $100,000 over budget. In its original form, the film ran about 75 minutes, and MGM prepared it for preview. (Plans for an elaborate musical score, with musical instruments representing each of the major characters, including a flute for Carroll, were scrapped - unfortunately.)

At long last, the preview night arrived - Friday, March 22, 1935 - a dream-come-true for Carroll. In her scrapbook are the ticket stubs from the big night, when *Mark of the Vampire* played to its first audience at Los Angeles' Uptown Theatre. Carroll attended with an old friend from San Francisco, who had become a publicist in Hollywood. She still laughs when she remembers his comment after the preview:

"Well - I don't think this movie will HURT you."

Variety's review, the next morning, was a bit kinder:

Spine chiller, produced to get gasps out of fans who like horror, Mark of the Vampire *fulfills its purpose despite a story that wouldn't hold water... Directorially, it's a nice job, with Tod Browning handling all the horror angles to get the maximum of squeals and gasps out of those who choose to be shocked...Carroll Borland, one of the cadavers, dead pans her way through the picture effectively...*

Back at MGM, there were concerns about the film's pace - such concern, in fact, that the front office ordered 15 minutes cut from the release print! For years, legend claimed that MGM cut the notorious "incest" episodes, which showed the illicit passion of the Moras, the Count strangling his daughter, and his bullet-in-the-temple suicide. Research disproves it; no such episodes were in the final shooting script, and Carroll says:

We NEVER shot those incest scenes everyone talks about; Lugosi and I could only suggest it in a handful of stills. The film never did explain why he had the bullet hole in his head. NEVER! It was my impression that Tod Browning was embarrassed, and not happy with the incest idea; he didn't want to touch it.

Cut from the film: an opening scene where the old witch (Jessie Ralph) beats her albino daughter for not keeping an eye on her cauldron; sunset at a farm, where the peasants beg Dr. Doskil (Donald Meek) not to leave them until the farmer returns home; peasant comic relief; a shopping trip to Prague for Elizabeth Allan; and much static dialogue. Carroll's only cut came in the introduction of the wizened little ghoul (James Bradbury Jr.), whom she and Bela's Count awaken at a window casement. Contrary to legend, MGM did NOT

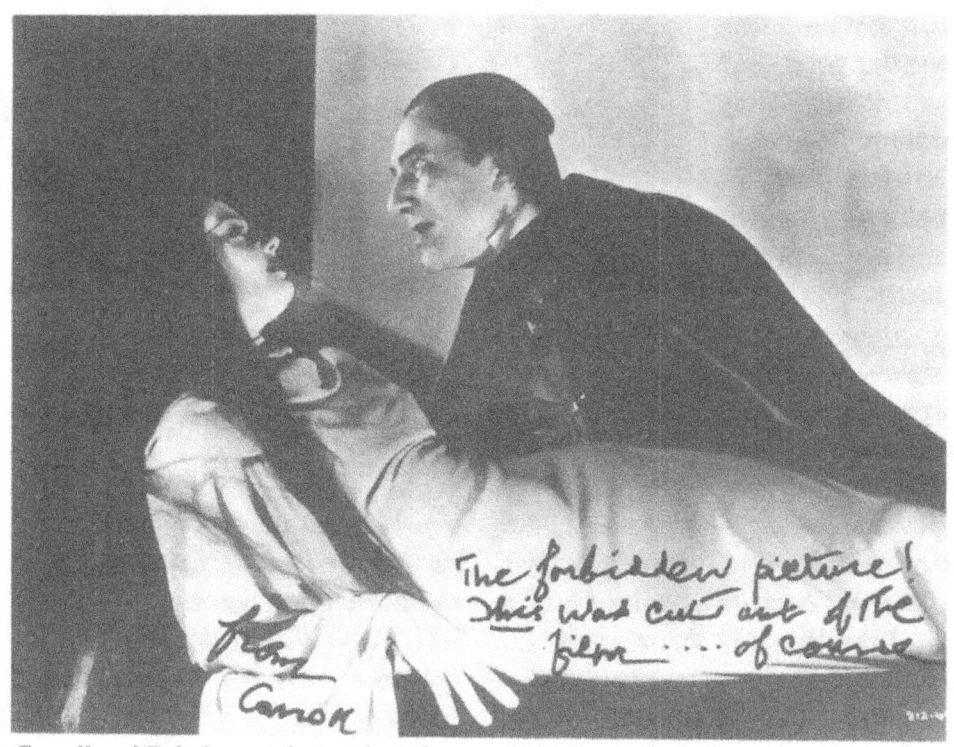

Carroll and Bela Lugosi during the infamous "incest scene" which was later cut before releasing Mark of the Vampire - from the collection of Charles Heard

29

cut the film to make it less gruesome, but truly, to improve the pace; when MGM was through with its cutting, *Mark of the Vampire* ran only 61 minutes.

"TOO MUCH HORROR FOR ONE THEATRE!" proclaimed the NY Times, when *Mark of the Vampire* enjoyed a show business distinction: a premiere at TWO Broadway movie houses - the Rialto and the Mayfair - on May 1, 1935. Weekly *Variety* took a new look, and reported:

A blood-curdler which deftly combines murder mystery, chiller and novelty elements...Bela Lugosi is particularly effective as one of the vampires roaming around the now-deserted castle, together with a couple companions, including Carroll Borland. Latter plays the girl of the old castle, dead 100 years, who returns to life at night in quest for blood. She almost takes the picture away from Lugosi on the chiller end, her performance being exceptional. Miss Borland's makeup is tops.

Universal's *Bride of Frankenstein* premiered at New York's Roxy Theatre just days after *Mark of the Vampire* opened - pitting Karloff's Monster vs. Lugosi's Vampire on Broadway. Business was good - and *Mark of the Vampire* ultimately earned MGM a profit of $54,000.

For Carroll, however, Lugosi's prophecy was true: a *Mark of the Vampire* curse seemed to loom over her, and her film career:

Lugosi was right - after Mark of the Vampire, *I was seen as a slinky vamp who couldn't read lines, and was good at haunting houses.*

It was a very strange thing following me: I had been a staff artist on the Columbia Broadcasting System in San Francisco, but because of having had no dialogue in Mark of the Vampire, *the word got out that I couldn't read lines. The voice was very important then - and the rumor was, "It's too bad the gal can't talk."*

I went on to land on the cutting room floor of several movies. I played an Eurasian in the Gable & Harlow China Seas, *and my part was cut. I was up for a part in MGM's* A Tale of Two Cities, *but that was scuttled. At Universal, I was up for* Sutter's Gold, *the part of Sutter's daughter, but again - due to the rumors started with* Mark of the Vampire - *this word went by that I couldn't read lines. I didn't get the part of the daughter in* Sutter's Gold, *but I did land the role of a Russian countess, a lovely section on the Russian river - and most of that was cut. I did see* Sutter's Gold *recently for the first time, and noticed that I did survive in it after all: in one scene, there I am, at the age of 21, sitting in a corner - eating shiskebab! Also at Universal, I was cast as one of the daughters of Ming the Merciless in the* Flash Gordon *serial.*

Dale is summoned before the high priest to prepare for her marriage to Ming. - Carroll Borland 3rd from right - from a Flash Gordon *serial - courtesy of Rick Atkins*

Mark of the Vampire *proved an oddly menacing picture for its cast. Lugosi was soon doing quickies, things on poverty row, Lionel Barrymore went into a wheelchair, Elizabeth Allan soon went back to England after she starred in* A Tale of Two Cities, *nobody ever heard of Henry Wadsworth again, and all of us took a terrible beating from that picture.*

Federal Theater Project, WPA - Up She Goes

Of course, over the decades, *Mark of the Vampire* would become a classic, and Carroll's Luna the classic female vampire. "It carried a SHEEN," says Carroll of the film; she would have to wait several decades for the film to receive its due.

Carroll went back to the stage. She joined the Federal Theatre, playing in *Everyman* at the Hollywood Bowl. (Irving Thalberg, MGM's "Boy Wonder" producer, came to a rehearsal one night in the rain, developed pneumonia and died shortly afterwards, on September 14, 1936). She played on the Los Angeles stage in such plays as *The Drunkard*, *Rachel's Man*, *The Women*, and *Russet Mantle*.

In 1937, Carroll married. Her husband is Vernon J. Parten, a newspaperman and publicist whom Carroll wed after a 6-week courtship. "He was a nice guy, and we got along beautifully," says Carroll of the man to whom she is still wed after 56 years. Together, Carroll and her husband wrote the scripts for the radio soap opera, *John's Other Wife*. Mr. Parten became the press agent for such stars as Marlene Dietrich, Humphrey Bogart, John Wayne and Sophia Loren.

Radio days - Carroll top

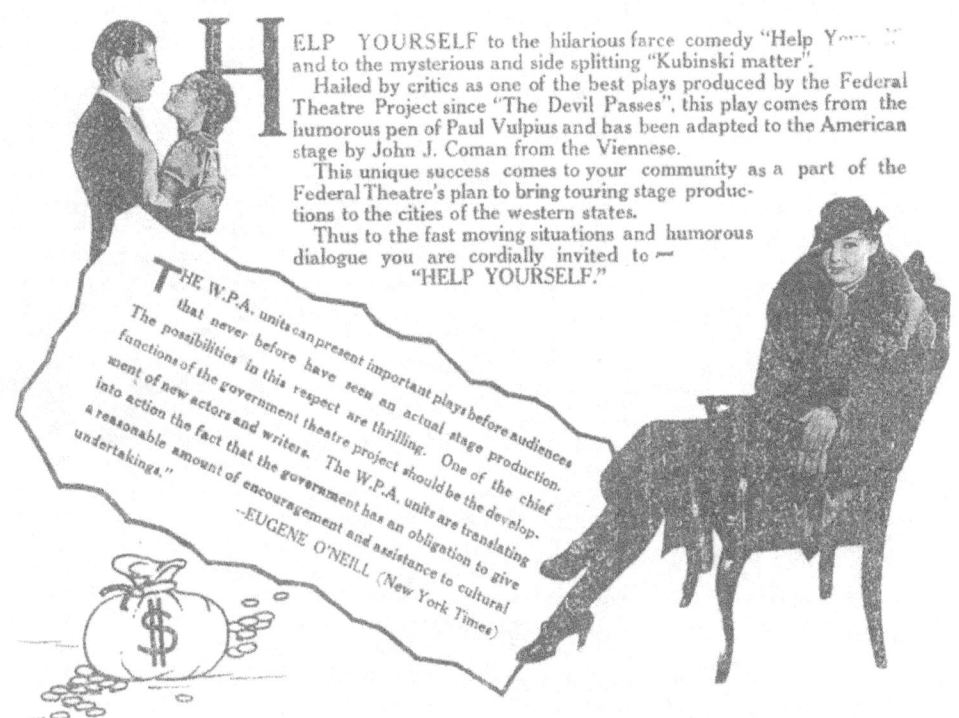

HELP YOURSELF to the hilarious farce comedy "Help Y...." and to the mysterious and side splitting "Kubinski matter".

Hailed by critics as one of the best plays produced by the Federal Theatre Project since "The Devil Passes", this play comes from the humorous pen of Paul Vulpius and has been adapted to the American stage by John J. Coman from the Viennese.

This unique success comes to your community as a part of the Federal Theatre's plan to bring touring stage productions to the cities of the western states.

Thus to the fast moving situations and humorous dialogue you are cordially invited to —
"HELP YOURSELF."

THE W.P.A. units can present important plays before audiences that never before have seen an actual stage production. The possibilities in this respect are thrilling. One of the chief functions of the government theatre project should be the development of new actors and writers. The W.P.A. units are translating into action the fact that the government has an obligation to give a reasonable amount of encouragement and assistance to cultural undertakings."
—EUGENE O'NEILL (New York Times)

Advertising for the Federal Theater featuring Carroll.

31

Carroll in Venice, 1949 - her favorite European City

Anne has understood perfectly her Mother's lasting love and affection for Bela Lugosi. Carroll told Charles Heard this story:

Anne was at Santa Cruz with Karl Malden's daughter, and she found that there was more status to being the child of an old horror film star than that of a TV personality. This seemed to irk Malden's daughter, Karla. One night, she greeted Anne at a party - "Oh, yes. I hear your mother was Bela Lugosi's mistress." Everyone got very quiet.

And Anne replied: "No, as a matter of fact, she wasn't, but I think she has never ceased to regret the fact!"

Carroll with daughter, Anne - March 1953

Carroll became fluent in four languages. She collected editions of Omar Khayam.

After World War II, Carroll and her husband lived in Europe for a while, in Paris and Rome.

Then, in her late 30s, Carroll decided she had another destiny to fulfill: motherhood. "My husband was opposed to the idea," says Carroll, "and I had to threaten to leave him." In 1952, their daughter Anne was born. Like her parents, Anne developed a fascination with the arts - and a familiarity with her mother's "other life" as Luna of *Mark of the Vampire.*

"I'm not afraid of vampires," said Anne when she was 12 years old; "my mom's one!"

Anne went to earn her Ph.D. at Yale in Classical Studies; today, looking very much like her Mother did in the 1930s, she is a lawyer who resides in Alexandria, Virginia. "Anne is brilliant, with an IQ of nearly 200," says Carroll, "I'm proud of her and love her very much. And she's given me two wonderful grandchildren!"

*Carroll, daughter, Anne and Forrest Ackerman
-courtesy Forrest J Ackerman*

As Carroll settled into motherhood, she had seen little of Bela Lugosi. In her Introduction to Richard Bojarksi's THE FILMS OF BELA LUGOSI, Carroll wrote:

I saw Bela Lugosi last on a late afternoon in 1948 or 1949. I was waiting for the light to change at the corner of Santa Monica and Sunset, when a car stopped with Bela in the passenger seat. He looked up and saw me, reached out his hand, as I did, but the light changed. His driver pulled away before we made contact, and although he turned and said something, I never saw him again alive.

Carroll has no regrets that she never married the domineering Bela; "I would have killed him, or he would have killed me!" she laughs. But she always loved him, and had followed the newspapers as they reported his many calamities: a 1953 divorce from Lillian, which broke his heart; a 1955 self-incarceration as a drug addict (stemming from a medical accident in the 1940s); his 90-day cure; and his 5th and final marriage to Hope Lininger, upon his release from the hospital. Drugs and alcohol had wracked Carroll's "friendly panther;" Bela Lugosi died August 16, 1956, in his Hollywood apartment, of a heart attack. He was 73 years old. As Carroll wrote to Charles Heard,

I knew that Bela had suffered dreadfully at the end of his life and I am glad that our time together was when he was soaring so arrogantly and liked him-self. He was a joy to be with, but he was such a panther of a person that he would be miserable if caged and made captive by dire circumstances.

Carroll went to the funeral at the old Utter-McKinley Mortuary on Hollywood Boulevard. She becomes emotional as she remembers the sight of Bela's body, dressed - as he had wished - in his Dracula cape:

I couldn't believe it. He looked so small in his coffin. He was a big man, but he seemed small - as though he had been shrunken by life. And he may have been - it was such a bad ending.

Although she attended the funeral, Carroll did not go to the burial service at Holy Cross Cemetery. Nor has she ever visited the grave.

"I like to think he might not really be there," says Carroll.

****

As a mother, Carroll became interested in Child Psychology. She took several courses - and decided to complete the college education she had interrupted over 20 years before for *Mark of the Vampire*.

A male education advisor counselled her NOT to go for it. She was almost middle-aged - and besides, such programs usually enrolled males.

"I didn't know testicles had anything to do with it," said Carroll.

Result: an outstanding career in Education. Carroll achieved an AA degree in Speech Arts at the University of California, Berkeley; a "Core Certificate" in Nursery School Education at UCLA; a Bachelor of Science degree in Human Development at Pacific Oaks College in Pasadena; a Master of Arts in Early Childhood Education at California State University; and finally, her Ph.D. in Education. As Carroll told the L.A. TIMES:

I'm living proof that a person does not have to stay locked in a mold that prevents further growth. In the course of life we should pursue as many careers as are needed to develop all of our potentials.

Carroll's many teaching positions include: Neighborhood Nursery School in Los Angles; Head Teacher at the Bethany Nursery Training School, Los Angeles;

Teacher-Director of the Barnsdall Park Co-op, Hollywood; Teacher-Director, the Los Feliz Co-op; Head Teacher, and Trainer, Head Start Pilot Program, Los Angeles; Teacher, Pacific Oaks Children's School; Teacher Trainer & Career Development Supervisor, Council of Mexican-American Affairs, Los Angeles; Child Development supervisor, Latin American Civic association; Faculty member, college supervisor for credential program and advisor for BA program at Pacific Oaks College; and Instructor for the UCLA Extension Division, W. Los Angeles.

The best thing I teach my students is to understand and appreciate the past, but always to look forward, at any age, to the experiences and knowledge that lie ahead.

All the while, Carroll never turned her back on her "other life," as Luna of *Mark of the Vampire*. She masqueraded as Luna for the Hollywood premiere of *The Tomb of Ligeia* (1965), where she was a guest along with Vincent Price, Elsa Lanchester and Vampira. For-

Carroll, Maila Nurmi, a passing ghoul and Elsa Lanchester - Tomb of Ligeia premiere.

Hollywood Tomb of Ligeia premiere
left to right - Carroll, Vincent Price, Maila Nurmi (Vampira) with Elsa Lanchester far right.

rest J Ackerman interviewed her for *Famous Monsters of Filmland*; the feature, "What Makes Luna Tick?", published in Issue #39 in 1966. Included in the interview was this story about Lugosi:

...he never was seen without his cigar...(but) he disapproved heartily of women smoking - he didn't think this was the thing to do, and so he didn't want me to smoke. He said, "Now, Carroll - now promise me you will not smoke until you are 20 - 21...I am very much against it, and if you take up smoking....I WILL HAUNT YOU!"

..But one evening, I was with a group of youngsters - I had just gone and started at Berkeley...I had a house party in the Santa Cruz mountains...we were all sitting on a balcony, so -

"Carroll, have a cigarette."

"No, thank you - I don't smoke."

...So they said, "Well, it won't hurt you to just light one, will it?"

And I said, "No, I suppose not." So I put the cigarette in my mouth, and they lit the match, and I was just holding it like this, ready to light the cigarette, and out of the night came a bat - knocking the cigarette right out of my hand!...I didn't smoke for years!

Carroll became a member of the Count Dracula Society. She followed the new Dracula films; when DRACULA became a Broadway hit revival in 1977, with the Edward Gorey set designs, Carroll attended a Los Angeles production. She admired Jeremy Brett's performance - "But I did regret the hot-cha-cha touches, trying to recreate the '20s and the Betty Boop overtones to Lucy." Of course, she also has taken note of the many female vampires of the decades who owe their original inspiration to her Luna - everyone from THE ADDAMS FAMILY'S Morticia to THE MUNSTERS' Lily, from '50s TV horror movie hostess Vampira to '80's TV hostess Elvira. Some years ago, Carroll was vastly amused when Vampira (Maila Nurmi) sued Elvira (Cassandra Peterson) - Ms. Nurmi claiming that Ms. Peterson had pirated her characterization.

"I get a kick out of the fact," Carroll told the press, "that those two are fighting over my face!"

Of all the actors who have played Dracula, Carroll has a favorite - George Hamilton. It was, of course, *Love at First Bite* (1979), and Hamilton's devilishness in the film was so much like Bela's that Carroll was amazed. One rainy Spring night, she drove into Hollywood...past the Utter-McKinley Mortuary, where Bela had appeared so small in his cape and coffin... past the Hollywood Roosevelt Hotel, where they had danced Viennese waltzes... past the old Hollywood Athletic Club, where Bela had lived in the palmy days... finally to a private theatre (where Academy nominations were being shown to members of the guilds), to see *Love at First Bite* on the big screen.

"I felt rather like a ghost," recalled Carroll. The audience was a young one; Carroll sometimes laughed at the "in-jokes" that the "infants" didn't understand. At the end, she wept.

After the movie, Carroll walked to her car. Later, she wrote her experience to Rick Atkins - who graciously has shared this letter for publication in this book:

I sat for a bit after the lights came up to reassemble myself. I came out alone and started back down Sunset to the place where I had parked. The crowd had thinned. The rain had stopped, but the streets gleamed like patent leather in the pools of light from stores and lamps. As I strode along, it seemed to me that footsteps were echoing mine, in a long, rhythmic stride. I lengthened my steps, as I so often had as we strolled on Hollywood Boulevard. It seemed to me I

could feel a touch on my shoulder, catch the aroma of a good cigar. In my mind a musical voice spoke:

THE VOICE: He was not bad, that young man.

ME: But how could he know?

THE VOICE: Know what?

ME: SO many little things. It was uncanny...Oh, I know you'll say, "He watched my films a dozen times, he's studied all my business, imitated my voice." But it was more than that. How could he know the little things? Did you know that when Lucy made her entrance, you would look at her with your face a formal mask, and then suddenly lift your left eyebrow?

THE VOICE: I did?

ME: You did, and a sigh would go out over the house like a wind before the rain. Especially on matinees.

THE VOICE: Ah, an effective touch!

ME: He did it. He looked at Lucy there in the disco, his face a blank, and then, his eyebrow rose. Oh, it wasn't just the voice and his "inky cloak, good mother..."

THE VOICE: You are still doing Shakespeare?

ME: No, listen to me . He HAD it. He had that devastating charm, the awful attraction of evil made irresistible, he had...

THE VOICE: (Laughing) I think I am jealous.

ME: No, you need not be. It was more. How did he KNOW? It was beyond acting, imitating, it was sort of possession...it was you coming through. I...I...it got to me. I could only think, with both in Love at First Bite *and the new staging of* Dracula, *that they now SHOW all the things we could only TALK about.*

The things which I first expressed in Countess Dracula, *the thing that made you want to play in it as a sequel. It is the sexual side, the passionate, the LOVE relationship.*

THE VOICE: It was always there when I played it, but we couldn't be explicit when I was alive.

ME: Yes, it was always there. That is why, some-day, I want to see Countess *put together on the stage. Do you realize, my ghostly friend, that it is now half-a-century since that story was written? Dracula disappeared, if you remember the lines, "Because you foiled me and cheated me of your mother, I was forced to lie as one truly dead for half-a-century..." which brought it up from the 1880s to the early thirties. Now, another fifty years has gone, do you think that again the story will start over?*

THE VOICE: As a comedy this time?

ME: Was BITE really a comedy?

THE VOICE: It was a good film.

ME: Oh, it was. As one of my friends said - you know, Eric, who has hands so like yours - he said, "This time, OUR side won."

THE VOICE: Then you liked it?

ME: All but the bats. They were so artificial. I think the ones in Mark of the Vampire *were much better. These just flopped, they didn't fly.*

THE VOICE: (Fading) But then, no one ever flew like you, my dear. And I, to quote Mark, *"Did you notice? I was the greatest vampire..." But he was good, very good, that young man. I think I would have to say, I like these new versions... Even if they make you laugh.*

ME: But at the end, I wept.

THE VOICE: (More faintly) But it was supposed to be a comedy...

ME: At the end, I wept. You see, I know what goes on behind that cape...

And we both laughed, and he was gone.

****

Recently, Carroll began sensing Bela Lugosi's presence. He came at night, and brought a message - the promise that *Countess Dracula* would be published.

On Memorial Day Weekend, 1993, Carroll Borland, although very ill with diabetes, and against her doctor's advice, flew across the country to Crystal City, Virginia, to be a Guest at the *Famous Monsters* Convention. The 3-day celebration honored Forrest J Ackerman, as well as Ray Bradbury, Robert Bloch, Ray Harryhausen, and many more giants of Hollywood Horror, Fantasy and Science Fiction.

Carroll with Bela Lugosi, Jr. at the 1993 Famous Monsters Magazine *Convention in Washington, D.C.*
- photo by Andy Hanson

There were talents from the Golden Age... Gloria Stuart, of 1932's *The Old Dark House* and 1933's *The Invisible Man*... Curt Siodmak, author of the screenplay for 1941's *The Wolf Man* and the classic novel *Donovan's Brain*... and Carroll Borland, from *Mark of the Vampire*. They were all there, representatives of over 60 years of Hollywood Terror all under the same roof, along with the daughter of Boris Karloff, the son of Bela Lugosi, the son of Dwight Frye, the great-grandson of Lon Chaney Sr. - and 3000 fans.

Carroll spoke on a panel with Gloria Stuart and Ann (*War of the Worlds*) Robinson. She signed autographs. She spoke with color and passion and humor about her infamy as show business's most influential female vampire.

And indeed, in the days following the convention, everything fell into place - *Countess Dracula* found a publisher.

Upon her return to California, she began preparations to publish her 60-year old *Countess Dracula* - and, in her words, "to send her flying into the night again."

****

Dracula, as played by Bela Lugosi, was a middle-aged, charming European gentleman. He had a certain sexually seductive quality for the millions of women who attended the matinees.

He also projected the seductive quality of death, but always death was overcome in the end. A stake was driven into Dracula's heart, and death was killed. Life went on, and real death remained a passageway to the Kingdom.

- Carroll Borland,
in an interview with *L.A. Times*
staff writer Bob Williams; *From a
Vampire to a Psychologist*

And, since Carroll's return home , the visits at night have continued from "my darling Bela."

The mist through the California valley, the fog from the Pacific...

"It's very vivid - I feel his presence," says Carroll.

Now every night, a tall man with the "profile of a hawk," in his dark evening clothes, appeared to Carroll. He promised her, gently, that *Countess Dracula* - the project that brought two passionate, brilliant, talented people together - would indeed be published. And perhaps he reveals, gently, comfortingly, that "passageway to the Kingdom..."

Through the fog, she sees the blue eyes of her "friendly panther," her "Pan," her Count Mora...her Dracula.

And in the night, she can see him smiling.

Carroll 1935 - photo by Jose Reyes

*Carroll and her "friendly panther," Bela Lugosi
publicity photo for* Mark of the Vampire

37

MARK OF THE VAMPIRE

Production Data

Studio: Metro-Goldwyn-Mayer
Producer: Edward J. Mannix
Director: Tod Browning
Screenplay: Guy Endore & Bernard Schubert
    (based on Tod Browning's original story,
    "The Hypnotist;" fictionalized by Edwin V.
    Burkholder; Additional Dialogue by H.S.
    Kraft, Samuel Ornitz & John L. Balderston)
Cinematographer: James Wong Howe, A.S.C.
Art Director: Cedric Gibbons (Harry Oliver & Edwin
    B. Willis, Associates)
Gowns: Adrian
Make-Up: Jack Dawn (William Tuttle, Assistant)
Film Editor: Ben Lewis
Recording Engineer: Douglas Shearer
First Assistant Director: Harry Sharrock

****

Original Budget: $208,734.01
Shooting Schedule: 24 Days
Shooting Days: 34 Days (10 days over schedule)
Starting Date: Saturday, January 12, 1935
Completion Date: Wednesday, February 20, 1935
Final Cost: $305,177.90 ($96, 443 over budget)
Cost for Cast: $64,000 (approximate)
Cost for Scenario: $20,049. 08
Fee for Tod Browning: $31,023.44

****

Length of First Cut: 6800' (approx. 75 minutes)
Length of Release Print: 5570' (approx. 61 minutes)

Premiere: Mayfair and Rialto Theatres, New York
    City, May 1, 1935.

The Players

Professor Zelen.............................Lionel Barrymore
Irena Borotyn.................................Elizabeth Allan
Count Mora...Bela Lugosi
Inspector Neumann............................Lionel Atwill
Baron Otto Von Zinden.....................Jean Hersholt
Fedor..Henry Wadsworth
Dr. Doskil...Donald Meek
Midwife..Jessie Ralph
Jan, the Butler.................................Ivan F. Simpson
Chauffeur.......................................Franklyn Ardell
Maria..Leila Bennett
Annie..June Gittelson
Luna Mora......................................Carroll Borland
Sir Karell Borotyn..........................Holmes Herbert
Innkeeper......................................Michael S. Visaroff
Innkeeper's Wife............................Rosemary Glosz
Englishman..Guy Belis
English Woman.................................Claire Vedara
Old Woman at Inn.........................Mrs. Lesovosky
Bit Man.....................................James Bradbury Jr.
Coroner...Egon Brecher
Sick Woman.......................................Eily Malyon *
Grandmother....................................Zeffie Tilbury *
Bus Driver..Baron Hesse *
Deaf Man...Christian Rub *
Fat Man..Robert Greig *
Card Player..Torben Meyer *

* Footage Deleted.

Box Office Performance

Domestic gross: $339,000
Foreign gross: $224,000
Worldwide gross: $563,000

Net Profit: $54,000

812-56

40

MARK OF THE VAMPIRE

Publicity Photos

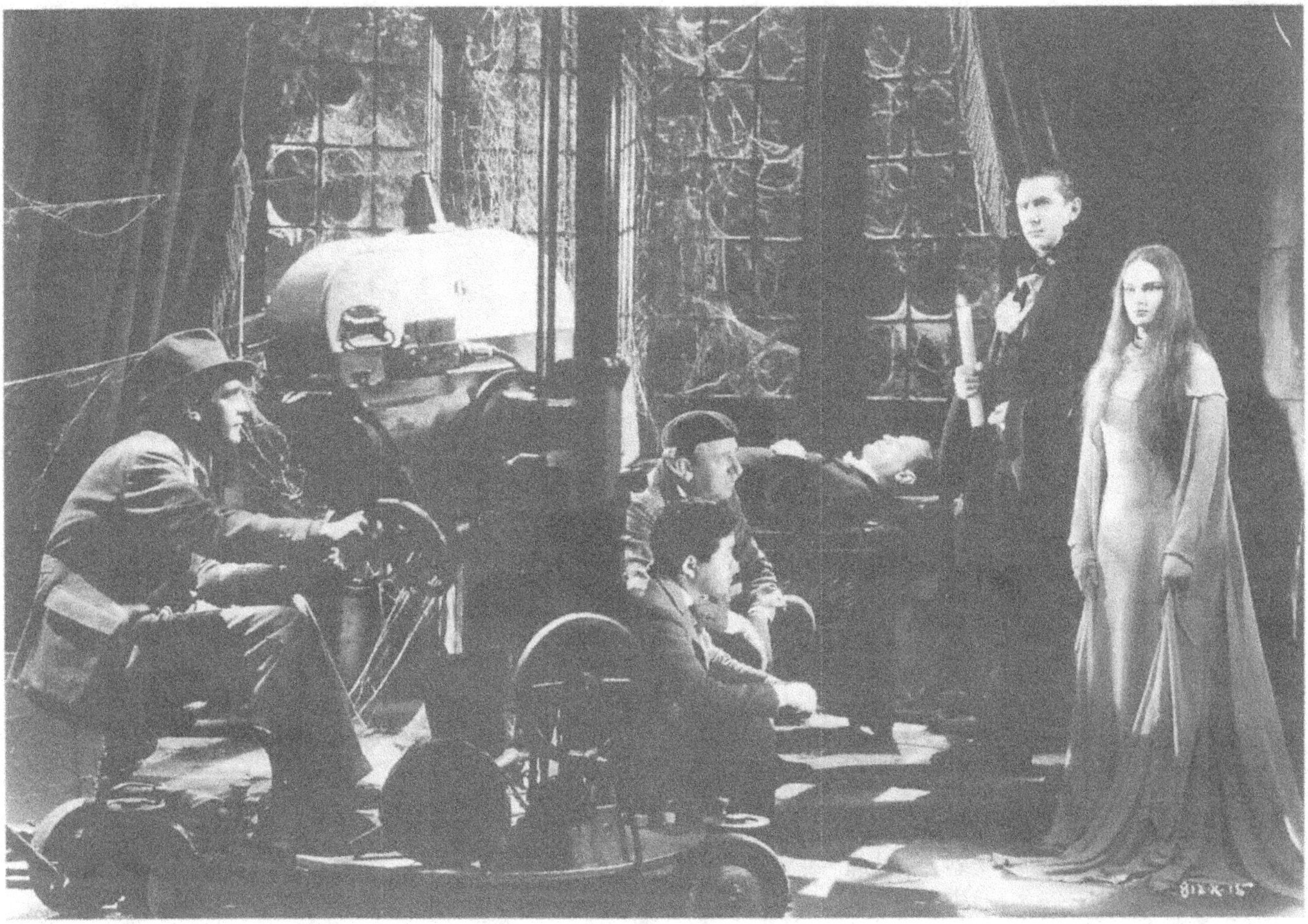

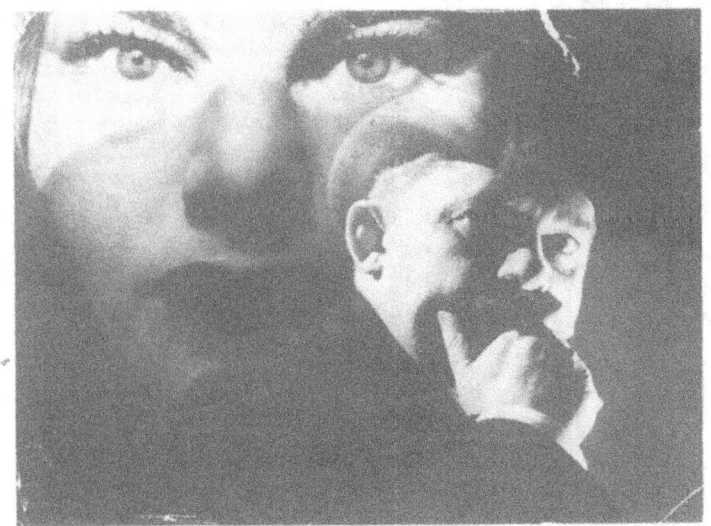

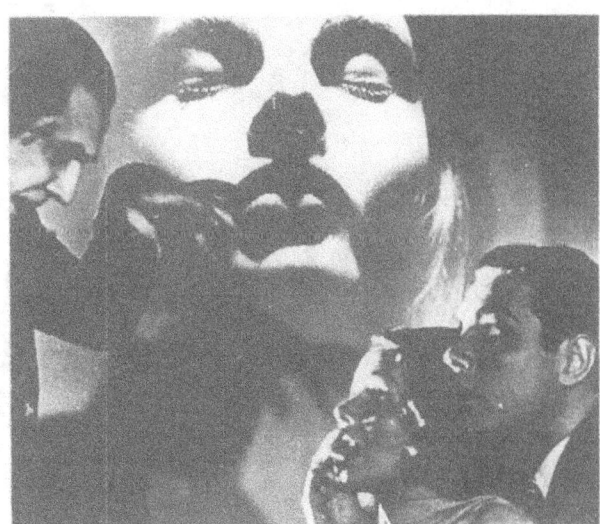

Carroll (right) with Elizabeth Allan

photo by C.S. Bull

*Cecil B. DeMille with Carroll -
1935 interview for* Delilah

42

In the dead of night, they braved the castle of nameless dread!

"It's the mark of the vampire!"

They brought terror to the living from the world of the "undead."

"Darling, no one--living or dead--will keep us apart!"

CINEMA

The New Pictures

Mister Dynamite (Universal). Because, like *The Thin Man*, this picture was adapted from a story by Author Dashiell Hammett, it will be billed as a sequel to that worthy prototype of this year's detective films. Because Edmund Lowe and Jean Dixon lack the nervous sparkle of William Powell and Myrna Loy and because the adaptation lacks the wit with which the earlier picture was written, *Mister Dynamite* suffers by the comparison it invites. Nonetheless, judged solely on its own merits, it is an engagingly light-hearted little study of crime and punishment, notable for bringing to the stage a detective at once more efficient and less affected than famed Philo Vance.

Kicked out of San Francisco for grafting, Detective T. N. Thompson (Edmund Lowe) is called back to help the proprietor of a de luxe gambling casino find out why two of his patrons have been murdered on successive nights. Handicapped by the interference of a pig-headed police chief, the chuckle-headed behavior of the gambler's daughter (Verna Hillie) and the readiness of his mistress (Jean Dixon) to act as straight man for his wisecracks, T. N. ("Call Me Dynamite") Thompson performs his task without drawing a long breath, except after some of his poorer jokes. Sample, to a butler who says his name is Quincy: "That's not a name, that's a disease."

Mark of the Vampire (Metro-Goldwyn-Mayer). When, in the gloomy Czechoslovakian village of Visoka, Sir Karell Borotyn is found murdered, with two ugly red marks on his neck and his body drained of blood, it tends to confirm the local superstition that his castle is infested with vampires. Later events are even more alarming. Sir Karell's handsome daughter Irena (Elizabeth Allan) is attacked by a glassy-eyed lady in graveclothes, who first puts Irena in a trance, then bites her on the neck. Irena's gallant young sweetheart is waylaid one evening by a mysterious what-not. When he wakes up there are spots on his neck also. These activities in *Mark of the Vampire* alarm Irena's guardian, Baron Otto (Jean Hersholt), cause a celebrated professor (Lionel Barrymore) to be called in to investigate. His theory: the bats seen flying about the countryside at night are really metamorphosed corpses whose murderous thirst for human blood is passed on to their victims. When it appears almost certain that Irena, overcome by ghoulish tendencies, is about to gnaw her fiancé's jugular vein, the police inspector on the case makes a remark which can be considered classic in its style: "There are things going on around here that I don't like."

Cinemaddicts who resent pictures in which supernatural goings-on are eventually explained as an elaborately arranged hoax will not be satisfied by the conclusion of *Mark of the Vampire*, which reveals the murderer of Sir Karell to be no bat at all but one of the humans in the story.

M-G-M's VAMPIRE
. . . from horror to hocus-pocus to hoax.

Up to this point, it is an engagingly whole-hearted combination of horror and hocus-pocus, characteristically handled by Director Tod Browning whose passion for gloomy lighting always leaves the impression that all the action has occurred in the cellar. Good shot: Lionel Barrymore expounding the powers of an herb called bat-thorn.

LOS ANGELES EXAMINER THURSDAY JUNE 20, 1935

BELA LUGOSI, Elizabeth Allen and Henry Wadsworth in "Mark of the Vampire," with Carol Borland in background, are in the new film at Pantages Hollywood.—Drawing by Ray Shuman, Examiner Staff Artist.

'Mark of the Vampire' Latest in Horror Cycle at Pantages

**from the scrapbook of
Carroll Borland**

OAKLAND GIRL'S STRANGE EYES WIN FILM POST

Former U. C. Co-ed Billed as "So Beautiful She Scares People" in New Movie Role

HOLLYWOOD, July 9.—Cinderella in a Nightmare—and "the woman so beautiful she scares people."

That's 20-year-old Carroll Borland, former University of California co-ed and daughter of Mr. and Mrs. Guy H. Borland, 2319 Park Boulevard, Oakland.

She's a Hollywood Cinderella because, as an unknown college girl, she sent her photograph and letter of application by mail to Tod Browning, Metro-Goldwyn-Mayer director, and got a job. That was in January of this year.

And as a result, now she appears as the weird "vampire lady" in "Mark of the Vampire," grisly nightmare tale of detectives and the "un-dead."

LIVED NEAR CHINATOWN

Her eyes did it. She had always been interested in occultism and things Oriental. Her childhood was spent on the fringe of San Francisco's Chinatown. There she roamed Grant Avenue, playing with Chinese youngsters and learning to know their ways.

Then someone noticed that her eyes slanted slightly.

"You've fooled around Chinatown so long that you look Chinese," her friends told her. But it was so—at least to a certain extent.

Here was a hunch; a great chance for stage success. Concentrate on the portrayal of Oriental characters.

PLAYED IN STOCK

Carroll prepared for her film career at the University of California by appearing in Greek tragedies, playing in stock during vacations and taking part in radio plays. She studied things Oriental. She collected the different translations and editions of Omar Khayyam. Mystery roles interested her.

She is a member of Delta Zeta Sorority. In 1934 Eva Le Gallienne offered her a place in her Civic Repertory in New York but she was unable to make the trip. In 1932 she won the privilege of taking part in try-outs with Bela Lugosi for a road version of "Dracula."

CO-ED 'VAMPIRE'

Carroll Borland, former University of California co-ed who plays the part of the "Vampire Lady" in the weird nightmare film, "Mark of the Vampire." She attained her role by simply writing a letter to a Hollywood director, enclosing her picture. The peculiar quality and intensity of her eyes won her a contract.

PACT OFFERED

CARROLL BORLAND, 20 year old film actress, whose contract with the Thelma S. Weisser Agency was expected to be approved by Superior Judge Marshall F. McComb late today. The agency asks permission to represent the actress in theatrical enterprises.

Citizen News, of L. A.
January 22, 1935

Thursday, May 30, 1935
OAKLAND POST-ENQUIRER says

RADIO WORK LEADS TO OPERA

By Paul S. Nathan

Down Hollywood way they have a pretty good working rule for thespians and writers who aim to crash the movies.

"Keep out of Hollywood," is the advice usually given. "Act a part on Broadway, sell a novel to a New York publisher, get a play produced. But steel clear of Hollywood, and Hollywood will start makin goffers."

You'll fin dan occasional exception to this rule. There's Carroll Borland of Oakland, for example, who went straight to the cinema city, put herself into the hands of an actor's agent and blossomed out with a feature role in "Mark of the Vampire," soon to be released locally.

But it's true that Hollywood is inclined to overlook the talent camped on its own doorstep.

And now it begins to appear that the road to operatic fame is equally roundabout, passing more and more frequently through the broadcasting studio.

COUNTESS DRACULA
a novel

by Carroll Borland

DEDICATION

To
A. B.,
from C.

Who is A.B.?
A friend.
Alive or dead?
With my friends, it's often hard to say.

-Carroll Borland

But oh! that deep romantic chasm
which slanted
Down the green hill athwart a cedarn
cover!
A savage place! as holy and enchanted
as e'er beneath a waning moon was haunted
By woman wailing for her demon lover!

-Kubla Khan by Samuel Coleridge

CHAPTER ONE

Clipping from the
Boston Post, June 15, 193___

Miss Marise Carter today became the bride of Mr. Anthony Morrow. The wedding was held at high noon in St. Paul's Church, Fr. F.G. Martin officiating.

The bride wore cream chiffon velvet, trimmed with pearls. The gown, modeled after the medieval style, set off Miss Carter's regal beauty admirably.

She is tall, with large dark eyes and blue-black hair that she inherited from her grandmother, the late Mrs. Concepcion Mendoza Carter, who was well known as a social leader during the last generation.

The lovely bride is a very popular member of the younger set, of which the groom is also a prominent member. She is a graduate of Mount Holyoke, and has spent the years since her commencement globe-trotting.

Mr. Morrow is a former Rhodes scholar. At present he is living in New York, where he is assisting his father in business.

The honeymoon will be spent in Transylvania and touring the Balkans.

ANTHONY MORROW'S DIARY

We left Munich at three o'clock in the afternoon and will reach Vienna early tomorrow morning.

Later

We stayed here in Vienna until five and then started out again. I can't say the Balkan sunrise is worth it. We will probably reach Buda-Pesth at noon.

Risa is enchanted with this country. She is perfectly happy here, enjoying the people, the travel, even the early rising...:and the hot food. The food is as hot as some of the applejack I've tasted in the Kentucky Mountains. Speaking of the Kentucky Mountains, there are as many feuds here as there are in the U.S.A. or in the Scottish Highlands. The Transylvanians, or rather the Wallshes, Dacians, Magyars, and Szekelys, have lived in this country for centuries, fighting their enemies the Turks for every inch of it.

This country we are going into is one of the few places where medieval superstitions still exist — pleasant thought! They even had the old system of feudalism until the war.

The people here remind me of a chorus from a Strauss operetta. The girls are rather pretty, but have evidently never heard of the boyish figure. They wear skirts with as much yardage as a good football game. The men wear big white pantaloons that remind me of one of the tintypes of the daring women of the nineties who wore bicycle bloomers.

ANTHONY'S DIARY continued
Buda-Pesth

This town seems to be full of elderly women and small dogs. The bitter-water springs outside the city attract all the dowagers that aren't busy managing the affairs of their young daughters.

This is the Grand Central Station of all Hungary, as all the trains center here.

Risa and I are going to the opera tonight. These people are passionate music lovers.

She has promised we would go with the Teldons on a hike up the Blocksburg. Why do I have to chase up a hill just to inspect an old, ruined, tumbledown fort? Kay Teldon has that ancient castle complex anyway! I could see that Bob didn't approve of his wife's idea anymore than I did. But what have we poor husbands to say about such things?

I've been looking over the map trying to figure out when we should get where. Tomorrow we hop to Klausenburg and from there to Borsa and through the Borgo Pass into Bukowania, then we double back to Dorna Vatra (I wonder who she was?), and then on to Bitzritz!

I hope Bob and Kay don't find any more ruined castles. This thing gets tiresome after awhile.

Incidentally, there are some of the funniest names here. These are a few of them: Maria-Threresopel (another she) Hodmezo-Vasarhey, Papa, and Brody. That last has too much of an Hibernian sound to fit into Transylvania.

MARISE'S DIARY

Oh, how I love this country! I love every inch of it, and I might easily say: "Where have you been all my life?"

I've traveled all over this world from Canada to Calcutta and from Alaska to Africa, but never have I found a spot that fascinated me the way this does. I wish we might stay here longer, but, of course, Tony has to get back to his business.

I am awfully glad I speak German. It has been such a help to me here. The people are so kind, so courteous and so patient; but, of course, German is not exactly their language.

I was so glad to see the Teldons. Kay can always find something interesting to do. Tomorrow we are going to visit the fort here. This is one of the spots that was so hotly contested with the Turks.

MARISE'S DIARY Continued

This city has almost as many statues as Washington, and many of them are of the heroes of ancient times.

There is one in particular that interests me. It is of a tall man, dressed in armor, his helmet at his feet and a drawn sword in his hand. He is beardless, with compelling eyes and heavy brows that nearly meet over an aquiline nose. It is executed in great detail, but with that total lack of perspective which characterizes the art of that period. It stands on a richly-ornamented base, on which one can barely make out the arms and the name:

Arpad, Voivode Dracula

Tony says I have the beginnings of a first-class antique collector. I would like to buy all the interesting things that can be found in the little shops here.

Now I have to go and coax an irascible hubby into exploring a fort.

ANTHONY'S DIARY

Up this morning and off for Klausenburg. The Teldons are going with us as far as Bitzritz, but we leave them there and go on into Bukowania.

The more I ride on these Hungarian trains, the more I long for the United States.

Of course, we could have come from Vienna to Buda-Pesth in three hours in a plane, but Risa insists on seeing the country, and of course, I must obey.

Later

Really, I think we have come to the jumping-off place. The train unsympathetically dumped us at Bitzritz, sailed off for Buda-Pesth, and left us surrounded by comic opera brigands. Risa, of course, was perfectly happy. How that woman does delight in cold water, hot food, and negative plumbing!

After we waved a fond farewell to the observation platform we had enjoyed for so many happy hours (?) we were hustled aboard a diligence, a sort of coach-like vehicle drawn by horses. I understand this affair is to take us over the hills, not to the poor house, but to Bukowania, oh ye gods!

ANTHONY'S DIARY Continued

Consarn Kay Teldon, anyway, and consarn Bob on general principles!

But first I'll explain how it all started. Risa saw another ruined castle on our way past Bukowania's frontier, and she indiscreetly invited the Teldons to dinner. We dined on "mamaliga," "impelata," and Medaisch wine. Of course Risa told Kay about the castle, and, of course Kay had to suggest an expedition. But here's where Bob comes in. He had the brilliant idea that we visit the place by night. Not such a bad idea at that. I thought Kay and Risa ought to stay at the inn, but nothing doing in that quarter. All I have to do now is to dig out my pistol and flashlight. I know we'll need the light, and as for the gun, there may be wolves or gypsies about.

MARISE'S DIARY

Back to Bukowania and to tell Kay about my castle. They have gone somewhere for the day, but we will meet for dinner. I have a letter here from Mr. Morrow, senior, who advises us to stay at "The Golden Krone Inn." His friend, Mr. Harker, of London, was in this part of the country several years ago, and has never forgotten it.

Poor Tony! I really feel quite a tyrant dragging him all over the Balkans — and he certainly is balking. No, that was not a pun, that was only a play on words.

The diligence was as jolty as a train, and, if possible, a trifle colder. We are still going eastward, and Tony says if we go much farther we will find ourselves in the west. He admits that he's awfully glad Christopher Columbus proved the world was round, otherwise he would be nervous for fear we'd soon be tumbling off the edge.

Later

I told Kay about my castle discovery, and we are going to explore it tomorrow night. Whoopee! That will be a real adventure. Tony tried to keep me from going, but nothing at all could keep me at home.

CHAPTER TWO

A fog was drifting in over the Baltic, a white blanket that covered the plains and hills and, then, growing bolder, carried its inexorable march up the mountain, feeling with opaque fingers for a foothold in the crevasses. It swallowed all that stood in its way, overwhelmed a peasant's hut, and changed a tall pine into a ghost that moaned with the voice of the wind. It even dared to rise and blot out the stars from the sky, and drown the moon in a misty sea. Upward and upward it carried its march, until the village of Bitzritz was engulfed in a tidal wave of woolly whiteness, and the oblong windows of "The Golden Krone" were mere fuzzy glow worms that clung crazily to a murky wall.

The fog reached the castle at the top of the hill. It wove through the tattered battlements and wrapped the crumbling towers in its folds. It brooded over the spot like a wraith of the Past. And one who watched could imagine seeing flitting shapes in the mist....of a man who passed through the heavy doors of the castle without opening them, and who was wafted to the topmost towers, and vanished, with the bats wheeling about him.

A cold night, a windy night, as dark as the deepest pit. Across the steppes were flickering blue fires, a will-o-the-wisp to lead travelers astray, and somewhere there was a green-gold glint or a distant howl that told of a pack of wolves.

Back at "The Golden Krone" there was music and dancing, for the townsfolk were doing the Czardgis to the tunes that Brahms made famous; those gay tunes with the underlying current of sadness that typified the life of the people — a life brilliant and colorful, but with depths of pathos and superstition.

High on a wall, gaily festooned with late flowers and autumn leaves, was a cross of mountain ash, woven with wild garlic and wolf bane. It was a charm to ward away the "vrolok," or werewolf, for this was Saint George's Eve when all evil was supposed to be abroad.

The gay quartet of Americans came trooping down and halted on the stairs to watch the dancing. The innkeeper bustled forward to ask their needs, but he stopped short when he saw they were dressed for the out of doors.

"But surely, meinherr, you aren't going out? But no... not tonight, of course, not tonight," he said with an air of finality. "Of course not tonight. Why, tonight is Saint George's Eve."

"Oh, I think I've got it," cried Kay Teldon. This must be some kind of a Balkan Halloween, and the 'goboluns'll get cha if ya don't watch out.'"

"Risa, really I think —" began Anthony, but his wife clapped her hand over his lips.

"Oh, we're not afraid," she laughed, pulling her dark wrap more closely about her. "The fog is lifting. See, there is a star."

The innkeeper's wife added her entreaties to those of her husband. "Madame," she said,

"I warn you as your mother might."

"Don't worry," laughed Kay. "I'll be Mrs. Morrow's chaperone. I won't let any sheik or warlock get near her."

But the kindly wife persisted. "It is not only the male you must fear. There is, it is said, at the castle, that which is worse: a woman — for a woman should give life, not take it — and when a woman is of the Devil, that is worse than the Devil himself."

"The female of the species?" quoted Bob. "Want to back out, anyone? Kay? Nonsense. Come along."

The innkeeper's wife shook her head direly.

Just as they were going out the door, she slipped something into Marise's hand. It was so dark that Marise could not see it, but she could smell it — garlic — and she smiled, for the Hungarian peasants believed that the "wampyr" or undead could not stand the scent of garlic.

"Whoops, my dear," chortled Kay. "I actually believe that old duck was thumbing his nose at me!"

"Nope, Kay, wrong again," explained her husband. "He was only warding off the evil eye."

"Brute, I knew I had a funny face, but I didn't think I looked like Ben Turpin," she snorted.

Marise shivered a little as she walked along, and not entirely from the cold. She was afraid of the wolves, and the fog depressed her.

Anthony, looking down, thought again how beautiful she was: the dusky tendrils of hair against her damp cheek, now rosy with the cold, her lashes studded with the glistening mist, and the small droplet that hid in the curve of her lip. He stooped and brushed it away with his mouth. Glancing up, she smiled and grasped his arm a little tighter.

It was so cold, she thought — that raw, damp cold that chills the eyeballs and makes the fingertips numb and aching. Absently she nibbled at the garlic as she went, welcoming the warm sting in her throat.

Soon the castle could be seen dimly through the mist, and Kay wondered audibly if they had elevators running to the towers.

"Really, I'm absolutely terror-stricken, aren't you?" she asked in a conversational tone.

"You sound it," jeered her husband. "Look, don't you realize that all old castles in Transylvania are haunted?"

"You're batty."

"Batty is right, Kay," called Risa. "The place is full of 'em. I could see them hanging in bunches as we went by. They will all be out tonight, so cold and slimy, brushing by your face, and rumpling your hair."

"Oh, yeah? Well, the first bat that musses this finger wave is going to join his bat ancestors, let me tell you."

"I can just see you chasing bats, Kay," announced Bob with an air of great wisdom. "They are only winged mice."

"Oh, Bob! I don't wanna go. I won't budge a step farther, and you can't make me."

"Aw, come on," urged Bob. "I'll keep the bats off you."

"All right," she quavered, "but if you let one touch me, I'm going straight to Reno when we get home!"

They hurried onward and soon reached the top of the hill, where, panting and laughing, they attacked the huge door of the castle.

Instinctively, they shrank back as a rush of cold, stale air met them.

CHAPTER THREE

As if their fire of enthusiasm had been quenched by the rush of wind, the four hesitated on the threshold.

"Gee, I always thought they had a skeleton in armor watching over these places," chattered Bob, "or at least they always have 'em in the movies."

"Y-you b-bet!" Kay made a gallant effort to regain her usual bubbling spirits. "I want my money back."

Little by little they ventured onward until they stood in the huge hall. The walls, made of great stones, showed gaps through which the fog trailed its silver veils. The portals were massively carved, but the figures had been almost effaced by time. The castle showed none of the delicate beauty that is so often seen in the buildings of France or Italy, but was rather of a rugged simplicity and a luxurious crudeness. There were none of the flying buttresses of the Gothic period, or the graceful arched ceilings. The roof was very high and beamed with heavy oaken beams. In fact, the whole impression was one of stolidity and heavy grandeur. The walls were hung with arras and tapestries of great age and beauty, which, though now faded and stiff with dust, still showed their former value.

At one end of the hall was a dais on which the lord and his guests had been want to dine, while opposite it was a huge fireplace with crane and spit. The black mouth of the chimney yawned eerily, and it was evident that the hearth had not known flames for centuries.

The floor was paved with flagstones and covered with rushes. Here and there were rude pieces of furniture: a chest, a bench or two, a long table that ran the length of the dais, and an odd throne-like chair that stood at its head. All the furniture was heavily carved and the upholstery of the throne was stiff with embroidery of gold and black and silver.

Over the fireplace was a shield carved into the wood, emblazoned with the arms of the lord of the castle.

"Throw your light up there, will you, Tony, there's a good boy. Hum — per chevron, sable, orr and argent. Why, Tony, where have we seen those arms before?" asked Marise in surprise. "I'm sure they are quite familiar."

"Let me take a look. Why, that's your old friend Dracula. You remember, that statue in Buda-Pesth, with the nasty expression."

"Tony, you are right. This might be the old castle of the Draculas."

"Yes, it probably is."

"Oh, gee! Come see what we have found," hollered Kay from the other end of the hall. "There's a staircase here bigger than the one in the Waldorf-Astoria. Let's see what is up on the next story."

"Bob, can you beat it, Risa has found the arms of her old friend Mr. V. Dracula. You remember the chap that looked like Noah Beery in one of his bad moments?"

"It did not," declared Risa warmly. "I think — well, I liked the statue."

"What? Tony? Going to let your wife be stolen by a grouchy-looking statue? And on your honeymoon, too?" teased Bob.

They were silent for a moment as they climbed the broad staircase, awed by the antiquity of the place.

"I feel as though I hadn't a right in the world to be here, as though I were desecrating the sacred loneliness of the place. It seems as though this castle has been asleep for a thousand years. We're so new and so cocksure of ourselves. This whole land is so old, so mellowed, one feels out of place here. It has cast a spell over me," mused Marise.

"What a sermon! Give us the benediction and let us depart. Where do we go from here, boys?" giggled Kay, who could never be serious for more than a second.

They opened a door and found themselves in an octagon-shaped room without any means of exit but the door in which they were standing. The walls were lined with books, and a lamp was burning on a table nearby. Bob cautiously stepped forward and took a book from the shelf. It was "All Quiet on the Western Front." He put it back on the shelf and started for the door. No one spoke, for the silence was electric with understanding. They trooped downstairs and were crossing the main hall when Tony cried, with a sudden note of fear,

"Where is Marise?"

The startled group looked at one another and then back towards the stairs. They started forward and then hesitated. Tony called, "Marise!" — but only the echoes answered him.

The silence was unbroken, except for a small choking cry from Kay. Bob turned pale with a sudden vision of dungeons and trap doors and hidden passageways and sliding panels acquired from the life of an ardent movie fan.

Then through the stillness came a sudden scream. It was Marise's voice, filled with terror and muffled with distance.

The three started for the stairs on a run, just as Tony's flashlight wavered and went out.

CHAPTER FOUR

While Tony, Bob, and Kay were exploring the octagonal room, Marise had softly opened a door into a room directly across the hall. This room had evidently belonged to the ladies of the castle, as it was furnished with more attention to bodily comfort than the others. The windows were curtainless and the dim light of the moon, which could now be seen through the thinning fog, revealed and yet concealed the vague objects in the room.

The walls were hung with tapestries and the floors were covered with soft rugs, which, at the time when the castle was in use, had been newly brought from the Orient. The gentle light streamed through the diamond-shaped panes, fell softly on the exquisite hangings, and partially hid the ravages of the moths, giving the tapestries the appearance of newness. In one corner was a small oaken table with an upholstered bench in front of it. Against the wall was a small couch that had evidently served as a bed, for it was canopied and piled with cushions.

Marise stepped softly across the room, and smiled to see her footprints left in the dust of the floor. She sank down upon the couch with a sigh, for the hike from the inn had tired her. It creaked under her weight, but it held. She leaned back against the pillows with an odd feeling of contentment and relaxation, watching the dancing particles of dust in the moonbeams that streamed through the windows.

Through the casements she could see over the whole valley. The distant hills seemed softened by the mellow light, and the towering mountains appeared to watch over the gorges with the benign air of an old and faithful guard with white hair. She smiled at the fancy and murmured to herself,

"Old Man Mountain..."

The fog had entirely disappeared but for a few vagrant wisps that lurked in the crevasses. The valleys and deep canyons melted into velvet shadows, and the light on the side of the mountain was as if some lady had thrown her glistening, gossamer scarf across them. The air was cool and sweet with the perfume of the night, and breathed peace like a benediction. The window was deep and the casement low, so that from her place on the couch, Marise experienced a feeling of freedom and expansion, even though she knew that directly under the window a sheer cliff dropped for hundreds of feet.

The dark was very friendly and comforting. Marise loved the dark. She thought of an experience in India, when the waving palms and the enticing night had called her from her bed to wander in the tropic darkness.

"I should like to live at night," she thought, "and sleep during the day. "I love the dark, love it, love it."

And then she screamed, for the arras had parted and revealed a tall man, clad from head to foot in black.

CHAPTER FIVE

For a long moment Marise felt that she would faint, but with a superb effort she regained control of her reeling senses and arose. The two stood in silence, and it seemed to Marise that her heart had stopped beating.

The man who stood in the doorway was so tall, taller even than Tony, she noticed vaguely. His face was of a waxen pallor, and his deep eyes seemed to burn with an unnatural fire. His hair and brows were dark, although he was slightly gray over the temples. He had thrown back the long, dark cloak he wore, and she could see he was in evening clothes.

He stood in the door as erect as a soldier, his head thrown back in an arrogant attitude. Marise shuddered as she noticed his mouth, so full and red and slightly open, showing the white teeth inside. He appeared to be a boyar, or lord, for his features told of his aristocratic origin. The high aquiline nose proclaimed him to be one of the Transylvanian mountain folk.

"Er — we — that is —" she stammered lamely, and then as her poise returned, she said, "We were exploring the castle. I have become separated from my companions. If you will pardon me —" and she stepped forward.

The tall man bowed and stepped aside. As she passed him she laughed a little nervously, for she wished he would say something. The silence was becoming oppressive. Instead, he drew back with a grimace. For a minute she was amazed, and then she remembered the garlic and smiled.

As Marise went down the stairs she realized that the man was following right behind her. She reached the lower landing, and smiled to hear Tony swearing in the dark. She flashed on her light and called:

"Here I am, Tony. What's the matter?"

"That's just what I want to know. Where were you? Why did you scream? Why didn't you answer when I called?"

"I was upstairs. I screamed because this gentleman frightened me. I did not hear you call." So saying, she stepped aside, revealing for the first time the man who stood in the shadows behind her.

Again the silence fell, and Kay began to giggle and cry at the same time.

"Shut up!" said Bob in a whisper. Then aloud: "I'm awfully sorry that we intruded this way. You see, we did not think for a moment that this place was occupied. We realized, however, that someone was around and we were just leaving when we missed Mar — that is, Mrs. Morrow. Of course, you will pardon me, or rather us, that is —" and poor Bob ran down.

"Of course," replied the man in black, with a bow.

"I am the, er — owner, and I was just making a round of the place. At present I am living in a restored part of the castle."

His voice, deep and compelling, fell pleasantly on the ear. He spoke in English, with a very slight accent.

"My name is Morrow," volunteered Tony. "This is Mr. and Mrs. Teldon."

The man bowed again as he said, "I am Dracula."

Kay Teldon lifted a small, scared, tear-stained face as she asked, "Are you any relation to the statue in Buda-Pesth, Mr. Dracula?"

"We are of the same family," he replied, with a smile.

"Are you the Count Dracula?" asked Tony, who had been making inquiries at the inn.

"Yes," he responded.

"A count? Why didn't somebody tell me?" asked Kay, extremely crushed.

"I believe you have seen most of the castle," said the Count, "or I would offer to show you around. The upper floors are not interesting, as they were remodeled several years ago, or at least, repaired."

"Do you live here alone?" asked Bob.

"Yes," he replied. "that is, since my sisters died."

"Oh, I am sorry," cried Marise, impulsively. "Did you lose them recently?"

"No," he answered, his deep eyes burning. "They died many years ago — or rather, they were murdered."

The little group started for the door, but stopped on the threshold, alarmed by the howling of the wolves in the courtyard.

"Listen, the spirits of the night. Our brothers." Then, noting the looks of surprise on the faces about him, the Count went on.

"You who dwell in the city cannot understand the feelings of a hunter. I love them, the children of the darkness."

"I wouldn't mind 'em either, if I had a good shotgun," muttered Bob under his breath. "Now how are we going to get back to the inn?"

"I will go with you. I am not afraid of the wolves," offered the Count.

"That is very kind, I am sure, but we couldn't impose upon you this way," replied Tony.

"I assure you that it is no bother at all, I was going out."

They passed once more through the massive portal and out into the clearing. All around them could be seen the glinting of the wolves' eyes, and in the darkness they seemed to be a bank of monster fireflies.

Stepping forward, the Count raised his arm with an imperious gesture. Silently the dark forms slipped through the postern gate and were lost on the shadow-clad steppes. Ever so often during the journey he repeated this gesture, and by the time they had come in sight of the inn, the howling had died into the distance.

Once, the Count left them and went off to the side of the road, following a flickering flame. When asked what it was, he explained,

"This has been the battleground of the Turks and our people for ages. Often during one of the forays, the townsfolk were forced to leave their homes. The safest way to hide their gold and jewels was to bury them. It is a belief that on St. George's Eve these blue flames mark the spots where treasure was hidden."

"But surely you don't believe that?" asked Tony incredulously.

The Count turned and looked at him for a long minute before he answered. "You would be surprised how many of these superstitions are founded on fact."

They went on in silence and when at last they reached the inn, the Americans entered and turned to the Count who stood on the steps.

"Good night, Count Dracula, and thank you so much. We really are very sorry."

"Good night," he answered with a courtly bow, and it seemed that a shadow passed over his face.

CHAPTER SIX

"What do you mean, Tony?" asked Bob, rather impatiently.

"Just that. He does seem to me to be the loneliest man I have ever seen."

"How do you know?"

"I really don't know. But somehow, he seemed to be quite disappointed that we didn't ask him in."

"This is a public house. He could have come in if he had wanted to," objected Kay.

"I know it, and yet, you know as well as I, that a man wouldn't spill out that about his sisters unless he had it bottled up within him so long that he needed to get it out for his own good. He was really glad of our sympathy. And, if you noticed, he didn't seem to be so angry about our butting into his home that way. He rather welcomed it. It was as though he was suffering and had to have some vent for his grief and anger. It must be a dreadful existence, alone that way, with only the bats and wolves for company."

"I guess you're right," agreed Risa, throwing her cloak on a bench before the fire. "It must be a solitary life."

"Gee," shuddered Kay, "I'd hate that. Just think, not a thing to do but read and eat and sleep."

"The thing that would trouble you, " her husband teased, "would be that there would be no one to listen to your wisecracks."

"And furthermore," Kay continued, with a glare at Bob, "we didn't see any bats."

"I suppose you're glad of that," laughed Tony. "Golly, you gave us a scare, Risa," he said, leaning over to kiss her. "Ooof! for the love a' Pete, woman, where did you get that garlic?"

"The innkeeper's wife gave it to me as we went out," she explained, "and I ate a little on the way."

MARISE'S DIARY

My, what a time we had the other night. That was exploring a ruined castle with a vengeance. I must say, I enjoyed it all. Even the Count was so nice. I liked him immensely. Or perhaps I better say that I was attracted to him. He was not at all likable, but rather, compelling and impressive. He seemed to lay a spell over me. I cannot shake off the feeling that came over me when he entered that room. He has an almost hypnotic power, with those burning eyes in that pale face. It is really odd that he should be so pallid and yet have such red lips. If he were a woman, I should be sure that it was lipstick. He is one of the strongest personalities I have ever known. I hope we shall see more of him. I think Tony didn't like him; he's almost jealous, I believe. Someone once told him that he, the Chrysler Building, and the Eifel Tower were the tallest things that were ever created — and the Count is even taller than Tony.

Later

We are going to see the Count this evening. He is sending his carriage for us at nine o'clock this evening. He has promised to show us the rest of the castle — that is to say, the parts we haven't already seen.

ANTHONY'S DIARY

What a crowded night that was! I don't think I'll ever get over the feeling I had when I saw that modern book in Bob's hand. And talk about a fright: my hair must have turned about three shades grayer when I found that Risa wasn't with us. Oh well, that's over now, but I was so interested in the Count. We are going back to the castle tonight, so Risa can see her precious room... and so the Count can see her. This is the twentieth century, and both Risa and I agree that jealousy ruins more marriages than incompatibility or cruelty. I'll admit that Risa is a lovely girl and just the type to attract a man like the Count.

That night at nine o'clock the quartet of Americans was waiting in the lobby of the inn. Just as the clock was striking, horses and the guttural voice of the driver were heard outside.

Someone rapped on the door with the handle of a whip. The innkeeper opened it, disclosing a tall man who seemed to be wrapped and muffled from head to foot in a huge great coat. He spoke a few words to the innkeeper, who turned to the waiting group and said:

"He says that the Count is waiting. The carriage is outside."

The four passed out the portal to the waiting vehicle. Marise laughed to see their breath hang like silver smoke in the air and their long, elastic shadows darting out before them.

They climbed in, the driver took his place on the box, cracked the whip, and they were away. Over the moon-flooded steppes they flew, like a dark blot on a luminous sea. As the horses clattered up into the courtyard, steaming and foam-covered, the driver leapt from the box and disappeared down a dark passage.

"Gee," sighed Kay, "look at that moon. It's too bright to be real. It reminds me of one of those sets where the hero is singing 'Meet Me In the Moonlight' in a high tenor voice, with orchestral accompaniment."

"I wonder what we're supposed to do now? I rather miss the brass band and the red velvet carpet," sighed Bob.

At that moment the huge door opened and the Count was bowing in welcome. The appearance was so sudden and noiseless, they were all startled. Absently, Tony noticed the black shadows do an about-face as the man in the door lofted the lighted lamp that he held in his hand. Just as absently, he noticed that no black pool streamed out from the feet of the Count; by some strange trick of light he threw no shadow at all.

They entered again in the great hall, this time lit with torches stuck in sconces in the wall. The floor had been newly strewn with rushes.

"Welcome to my poor house," said the Count in his deep, rich voice.

He escorted them up the broad stairway into the octagonal room, where a huge fireplace lit the corners with its crackling blaze. One could see that the fire was newly made, for the top logs had not yet begun to burn.

On the table was wine and the small current cakes so familiar to the Balkans. All the service was very rich: the bottles and plates were of gold encrusted with precious jewels — amber, opal, garnets and chrysoprase — which reflected the dancing firelight. Marise could not repress a cry of joy and surprise at their richness. As Kay said later, the jewels were as bright as the port and starboard lights on a boat.

The table was spread with a tapestry of amazing age and beauty. Tony remembered seeing a similar one in the Carnegie Museum, but in no such state of preservation.

Seated in the heavily carved (and in Kay's opinion "darned uncomfortable") chairs, they drank the wine and nibbled the cakes. The Count refused to touch anything, however, saying that he never ate at night.

For many hours they sat there listening to the Count tell of the wars with the Turks and of the legends of the country.

"Many were our heroes," he told them, "and many are forgotten. The men of our family led them. Often we crossed into Turkish land and over the great river. Again and again we were beaten back, leaving the bloody fields in defeat, but as many times as we returned, for we had the ages in which to fight, and only we could ultimately triumph. One of us, called Voivode, the leader," — here Marise glanced up with a smile, thinking of the statue — "crossed into the other lands and carried away much of the Turkish treasure."

Tony glanced down at the bottle from which the wine had been poured. It was of ivory, with that minutely delicate carving particular to the Orient. Dracula followed his glance and replied to his unspoken question.

"That bottle," he continued, "that bottle was won with great bloodshed and loss of life. It is a symbol. We went into the East and took from it the best.

"But come now, I have been a thoughtless host to let you sit here and listen to my ravings and boasts of my family. Would you like to see the rest of the castle?"

"Oh no, I'd rather listen to you," cried Risa.

"Thank you," he replied with a bow.

"We really don't want to bother you," put in Tony with a frown. "You see, we might get separated again."

"If you don't mind," began Marise hesitantly, "I should love to see my — the room again."

"But certainly." And the Count rose and led the way across the hall.

"Let's go," piped Kay. "You see, we didn't get a chance at that room the other night."

They crossed the wide hall, swung back the great door, and, parting the arras, they entered the ladies' room. Marise's footsteps could be seen in the dust of the floor, and the window was still open.

"It wouldn't take a Sherlock Holmes to tell what happened in this room," laughed Kay.

"Look," said Risa from the casement. "It will soon be morning."

"Oh, I am sorry," said the Count. "I have kept you too long. I will call my coachman."

In a minute the Count returned and informed them that the carriage was ready. They followed him down the stairs and through the great hall. At the door he bowed, and, bidding them good morning, disappeared.

Soon the coach drew up and they entered it, to be whirled off over the steppes.

"Gosh, here's your hat...What's your hurry?" gasped Bob. "Some speed, this."

"I wonder," mused Tony as the coach slowed down in front of the inn door, "why he didn't wait until the carriage came, and see us off? Why was he in such a hurry all of a sudden?"

CHAPTER SEVEN

The next evening and the next were spent at the castle on the top of the hill. The hours passed quickly as Marise, Tony, Kay and Bob listened to the Count's vivid tales of the border. He painted the picture of the old days for them with a sure hand, and out of mere words called before them the times when the name of the Draculas was a byword in the country, symbolizing all that stood for strength and power. The Americans understood some of his pride in family that comes only after generations of ruling.

"Here we are boyars," he would say, "here we are the lords. I would not leave this country, not for anything that could be offered."

But most of all, the Count loved to dwell on the heroism of the men of his family. He swelled with pride as he told them of his great ancestry.

"And there was ever a Dracula at the head of the expeditions across the wide water. We were the leaders."

Thus would the four stay spellbound as his hypnotic voice and charming manner wove about them a spell of unreality. But always he would break off at an hour or so before dawn, and, bowing low, leave them at the foot of the stairs. The coach took them swiftly back to the inn, left them, and vanished into the darkness.

"That guy gets mighty anxious for his sleep about the same time each morning. And isn't he the conceited old duck? When he gets going on his forefathers, nothing can stop him. Did you notice the way 'we' did this and 'we' did that? He sounds like Lindberg — and if you ask me, he'd have liked to say 'I'," remarked Bob after such a night.

"Come on, now, you're jealous 'cause you can't even remember your father's middle name, much less your grand dad's first one. Now why didn't I marry a man like that? Why, I might have been a Lady today," jibed Kay.

"I doubt it. Not even marrying a lord could make you one," returned her husband as he hastily ducked.

"Did you notice that look of disquiet and dismay the Count assumed when you dug out your compact and admired yourself in the mirror? You ought to realize that here on the continent 'we noblemen expect a woman to always be a lady'," Bob said with an exaggerated drawl that would have infuriated Kay, if she'd heard it. She had, however, already entered the inn.

A few minutes later, as Marise was brushing her hair, she called to Tony, "Tony, don't you think we should ask the Count to go with us on our expedition into the mountains tomorrow? We've been up at the castle so much lately; we should do something to return his kindness."

"Go ahead," called Tony from the other room. "You write him a note and I'll drop it tomorrow on my way by the castle."

"I will, Tony. Turn out the light as you come to bed."

LETTER FROM MARISE MORROW
TO COUNT DRACULA

My dear Count:

The Teldons, my husband, and myself are making an expedition into the mountains tomorrow at ten o'clock in the morning. We would be very pleased if you could accompany us. We start here from the inn on horseback. As we will pass by the castle, you could join us there at half passed ten.

Sincerely,

Marise Morrow

That evening the three Americans were seated on the broad porch of the inn watching the sunset. The mountains seemed to melt into the violet shadows that were stealing down the slopes and encroaching on the last golden spears of sunlight. The son of the innkeeper was seated on a balcony above them, singing softly to the accompaniment of his mandolin-shaped instrument. The sleepy cooing of the doves could be heard from the barnyard, and the weird call of an owl echoed from the distance.

The lingering pools of light struck a responsive note in Kay Teldon's red-gold hair, as if they hated to leave. The huge crimson sun finally slipped behind the mountains, dyeing their snow-crowned summits all the colors of the rainbow and flooding the crevasses with prismatic lights.

Marise leaned back against the pillar of the porch and sighed. She hated the thought of leaving this country where she was so happy.

"Just one week more," she sighed miserably, "then back to civilization."

"What are we going to have to eat tomorrow?" asked Bob, ever mindful of the inner man.

"Just enough, Big Boy," returned his wife. "If you don't look out, that tummy of yours will be a bay window by the time you're forty."

"You should worry," retorted Bob, "it won't be your bay window."

"That's right. Fat men usually have thin wives," laughed Tony.

"Ooooo! Look who's coming," chortled Kay.

Along the trail that led up the mountain, they could see a horseman riding quickly. As he rounded the bend, one could make out the features of the Count. He was mounted on one of the huge black horses that reminded one of the chargers of the Middle Ages. He drew up at the stairs of the inn and dismounted. It was the first time they had ever seen him out of evening clothes, and the smart riding togs made him appear less tall than usual.

"Good evening," called Tony, descending to meet him.

"Good evening," he replied. "I have come in response to the so-kind invitation of

Madame Morrow. I regret extremely that I will not be able to accompany you tomorrow. I have business in Buda-Pesth, and must be absent for several days.

"Oh, we are so sorry," replied Marise. "Will we see you again before we go? We are leaving in a week."

"But certainly. I am only to be gone for three days. We must have another evening together before you depart."

So saying, he mounted, called good-bye, and galloped up the hill.

"Well," remarked Bob as he faded from sight. "I certainly take off my hat to the old duck. He can ride like Gibson. Though I won't be sorry to miss a day of ancestor worship, I'd like to watch him ride. He seems like part of the horse."

"Perhaps if you watched him long enough you might be a better rider yourself," murmured Kay sleepily from the shadow. "You ought to have seen Bob at home trying to play polo. He was tall, and so was the horse, and the mallet was so short, you could see daylight between him and the saddle every step the horse took. He bounces so prettily 'cause he's rather fat, you know.

" Yep, if you watched the Count long enough..." and the rest was lost in the distance, for Bob had picked up his small wife and carried her into the inn, much to the amusement of the Morrows and the surprise of the innkeeper's wife, who shook her head in despair over the 'crazy Americans'.

For an hour or more, Tony and Marise sat on the moonlit porch, watching the bats wheeling above the turrets of the Castle Dracula, and listening to the mournful cry of the wolves. When at last Risa went to sleep with her head on his shoulder, Anthony, too, wished that he need never leave the country.

CHAPTER EIGHT

August 28,
Boston, Mass.

Dear Son:

We were all so glad to hear from you, and pleased to hear that you and Risa are having a good time. I have found just the house for you, out in the suburbs. It has a wonderful view — that is, it will have when they get in the scenery. From the letter your mother received from Risa, I gather she'll never be satisfied with Boston again. Tell her to bring home one of the Carpathians. She will need it to put outside the dining room window.

I gather from your itinerary that you will be leaving Bitzritz in about a week. I wonder if you could manage to stay over for awhile and go to Bud-pesth for me. I want you to interview Herren Klopstock and Billreuth, the bankers. It is much better to have you interview them personally than it is to write. As you are so near to them, I am sure you will not mind doing this for me. I know that Risa won't mind staying an extra week.

So you ran into the Teldons. That is odd. Europe is a large continent. Even for you fool kids.

Give my love to Risa.

Your affectionate

Dad

ANTHONY'S DIARY

Hooray, a reprieve. Dad wants me to do some business for him in Buda-pesth. Talk about luck! — this takes the cake. I must say, I sound like Kay Teldon, but both Risa and I are so glad that we don't have to leave this wonderful place at once.

Since Dad has given me an excuse to stay here for another week, we are going to double it and stay a fortnight. I'm afraid if we stay much longer we'll have to buy another trunk, as Risa has bought pottery and yards of embroidery from the peasants.

If I go to Buda-pesth, I may see the Count. He said that he would be there for about three days. I hate to leave Risa alone here, but she says she prefers it to traveling down to the city with me. At least she will have the Teldons for company. I hope they don't go to the castle if the Count gets back before I do. I'd hate to have her go up there without me. I don't know why I feel that way, but I do.

Well, there's always packing to be done, if I'm going to Buda-pesth for Dad.

I won't leave until tomorrow, as I don't want to miss the trip into the mountains.

I thought Risa was going to die of joy when she found she didn't have to leave her precious country.

We had a fine trip up the mountains on mule back — I can see now what Kay meant when she said that her husband ought to watch the Count. I was afraid Bob, Kay, and Risa were going to have hysterics when I finally got on that mule. He was so little, it broke my heart to think of riding him. After I mounted, I must have looked silly, with my feet hanging down and just about tripping both of us. It seems brutal to make such tiny beasts carry such burdens. Actually, I felt as though every rock sheltered an irate member of the S.P.C.A.

When we reached the summit we were all as hungry as bears. The lunch basket looked as though a typhoon had hit it when we got through.

After we reached the top of the mountain we found it well worth the climb. We could see far over the forests and out onto the steppes beyond. The trees seemed to be marching up the heights and battling for their existence at the snow line. It must be wonderful to fly over this country and see it stretched out under one like a great relief map. The view we got from the mountain was enough to promise that.

For an hour or more we rambled around aimlessly, gathering the edelweiss and getting our fingers frozen with snowballing, when Bob began to make those hungry noises peculiar to a hungry male. Then came the hunt for the lunch basket. High and low we hunted, but it had absolutely disappeared. We clambered up on the rocks and peeped down the crevasses, while a superior donkey wagged a knowing ear at us.

Bob made a remark to the effect that horse meat salami was very good, and Kay suggested that if worst came to worst, we could eat the dog. This last remark caused said dog to lift his nose in the air and give vent to a soul-rending wail. He dashed around the side of the mountain in search of his master, our guide. I suppose it was the primeval hunting instinct, but Bob and I tore after him. What should we find on the lee side of the mountain but our guide and the missing lunch basket, the former trying to get away with a cold chicken at one gulp! The dog sat down beside him and cocked his head on one side as if to prove to us that he had found the lunch and it was not now necessary to dine on dog meat.

That evening as we were scrambling down the mountain, I could not help comparing our rickety cavalcade and uncertain horsemanship to the wonderful command of the Count over his mount. I heaved a sigh of relief as we reached the foot, and wondered how we had managed the descent. Tired and disheveled, we arrived at the inn hungry, even though earlier we had dined so heavily on eggplant stuffed with paprika and fritters of hot cornmeal.

I noticed that Risa looked pale and worn. I hope that this trip hasn't tired her.

ANTHONY'S DIARY Continued

I am not going to Bud-pesth today, as Marise is not well. She woke this morning with a bad headache. She urged me not to put off the trip to the city.

Bob and Kay are hanging around the door in hopes that someone will suggest something to do. The whole place is so quiet, it reminds one of a hospital. All the people were sorry to hear that Marise was ill.

Evidently Bob woke with a stomachache this morning, for he was so very quiet. So unusual in Bob. I will admit it hasn't been very lively; we were afraid of disturbing Risa. We sat on the porch in the sunshine and read. Bob drowsed over an illustrated paper, Kay poured through some French fashion magazines, and I read an old book of the innkeeper's: Abbe Calmet's "Dissertation on the Vampire." What a morbid old duck he must have been! It is an awfully scary book, and although I'm strong-minded, I don't think I'll like going to sleep tonight.

I'd like to see Kay meet a bat after reading that book. If she was afraid of them the other night at the castle, she would pass out now. Oddly enough, there's a huge bat circling around the moon as I look from my window...

ANTHONY'S DIARY Continued

Marise is no better. She caught a slight cold in the snow, day before yesterday. There is no cause for worry, and I am going to Buda-pesth tomorrow. She was angry yesterday because I did not go, saying she wasn't going to let me hold up my business because of her.

There is one thing, however, that makes me anxious. Last night she rose from her bed and walked across the room to the window. Although it was wide open, she made a motion as if she were lifting the casement. I called and asked if anything were the matter, and when she did not answer me, I rose and went to her. I was surprised to find her sound asleep. I led her back to bed, and she got in quietly. She did not stir again all night, and when I told her about it in the morning, she said that was the first time she had ever walked in her sleep. She did not remember any of the events of the night before, or any of her actions, but attributed them to the fact that she had had bad dreams. I was rather afraid she might have caught more cold.

ANTHONY'S DIARY Continued

Well, off at last. I did not like to leave Risa but she insisted that I go. I think I'll ask some doctors if there is anything serious the matter. I shan't tell her, as it would only make her angry if she thought I was worrying. No one knows how glad I am that the Teldons are here. The Count will be leaving Buda-Pesth just as I arrive. I don't think that they will go up to the castle without me, as Bob doesn't think very highly of the Count, anyway.

If I get Dad's business done well — who knows? He may make me junior partner when we get back.

MARISE'S DIARY

I sent Tony off at last. He argued like a small boy on the way to the dentist. There is nothing wrong with me.

He surprised me when he said I'd been walking in my sleep. I have never done anything like that before. I was having dreadful dreams.

It seemed that somewhere Something was calling. I had no choice but to obey. It was so hot — stifling in my dreams — I tried to open a window. The Something was coming nearer. I was not afraid; I moved forward to welcome it. I could feel a strange presence. A compelling presence. I still think that there must have been someone outside. The impression that I was not alone was so strong, I still cannot shake it off.

For a short time I was at peace with Him. Then I heard Someone else calling me. I left my Master with a feeling of regret, of expectations that were unfulfilled. I did not want to go. The second voice was stronger than the first. I could feel hands upon me, leading me. The second being was Tony, probably, but the first... oh! It was all imagination.

We have arranged for Kay to sleep in Tony's bed while he is gone. I did not want to bother her, but Tony seemed so worried.

MARISE'S DIARY Continued

When we went to bed last night Kay insisted on locking all the doors and refused to open a window. She is so timid for one of these "modern women." She said that about one o'clock, I arose and went to the window to open it. She woke up and led me back to bed. This time I almost "got away with it". The window was halfway raised. Kay told me that once she had me quiet again, she closed the window. She even shuddered next morning as she described the great bat she had seen outside. The bats of this country are not so very big, and I don't imagine that they frequent the more closely-settled spots. She assured me, however, that this one was a giant, and that he was so near, one could see his big red eyes, "like the Count's," she said. A great compliment for him!'

I don't like this idea of taking these midnight excursions. Oh, I can't help it, I have an awful presentment of danger. I wish Tony would come back. I need him....

MARISE'S DIARY Continued

Last night I had the most amazing experience... or did I? I sit here in the warm sunshine of morning, sipping my coffee and eating Alma Torte, and wonder if I'm sane. Or as Kay put it, "Do we call in a psychiatrist or the Society of Psychic research?"

I shall try to record my experience as factually as I can.

Last evening, as the moon rose, the three of us — Bob, Kay, and I — walked up the hill to the castle. As usual, the Count met us at the door himself and escorted us to the octagonal library. After we were settled around the fireplace, he excused himself, explaining, "My servitors are rude and unprepossessing. I prefer to wait upon my guests myself." This is his custom, but it seemed he was gone for longer than his want. Talk died down, and Bob seemed willing to sit in silence and watch the cities in the coals. Kay seemed rather bored, so I suggested that we take one of the candles and see the view from the tower room. I thought that the moonlit forest must be lovely to see from that height.

"Oh, go along," said Bob. "I'm sure the Count won't mind. I'll wait here and tell him where you've gone."

I took the candle and Kay and I started across the long hall to the solar or tower room. At the door, for no reason at all, I lifted the light and looked down the hall. It was then I saw her. A woman stood at the foot of the hall, her gown gray against the stone. I know that Kay saw her, too, for when we compared notes later, her description was the same as mine.

Her face was luminously pale, framed in long dark hair. She was slim, and carried herself like the caryatid from some classic temple, but I had the feeling that she was immeasurably old. Our eyes locked, and it seemed that she gazed at me with hatred... and was it sorrow?

I could feel Kay's hand tremble on my shoulder, and even as the candle wavered in the sudden cold wind, the gray lady was gone. Or was it merely a wisp of fog that drifted off?

With unspoken consent we turned and hurried back to the light and warmth of the library. The Count was just setting down a tray of small cakes and glasses, golden with Takay. I wouldn't have told him of our vision, but Kay, of course, had to blurt it out. He seemed frozen for a moment, locked in the posture of leaning over the table. I saw his hands tighten on the tray so that the knuckles ridged, and it seemed the red of the fire danced in his eyes. But when he straightened up, he was smiling.

"This is a very old habitation," he explained. "Many strange and violent events have taken place here. They say that disturbed spirits linger in such places. Who knows? She may have been some ancestress of mine."

"Do you mean a ghost?"

The Count handed Kay a Venetian goblet of the wine. "Doesn't your great poet say, 'There are more things in heaven and earth than are dreamed of in all your philosophies.'?"

"I wouldn't know," Kay answered. "I flunked English Lit, but this old pile really does have everything, even a built-in ghost."

The Count turned with a glass for me. More sternly than I thought the occasion called for he asked:

"I hope you were not disturbed, Madame?"

I took a sip of the sweet wine and shook my head at him over the rim of the glass. "Startled, I admit. She seemed so real... so sad."

"Your heart is tender." He smiled, but his eyes were hard, and I was glad when Bob changed the subject.

Today, as I write these words, I am convinced that Kay and I were victims of an hallucination. Is it not possible that we felt called upon, alone, at night in a medieval castle, to see some such apparition? Really, I do make myself sound like some heroine in a Gothic novel, or the first act to "Lucia di Lammermoore." Or, as Bob said, "Just put it down to too much paprika in the Bableves Csipetkevel, if you can pronounce it."

I'll try.

LETTER FROM KAY TELDON
TO ANTHONY MORROW

Dear Tony:

I know that Risa would be wild if she knew I was writing to you. I wish you could pack up and return as soon as possible... She would not want me to bother you for the world, but I really am anxious. There is nothing especially wrong with her, but she is walking in her sleep again, is so pale, and the lack of rest is telling on her. We both are afraid of something we can't explain and wouldn't confess to each other for anything. I know I sound like a hysterical old maid who has found a burglar under her bed, but please, if for no other reason than that of auld lang syne, take a tip from the wise, a load off my mind and Come Back!

Yours,

Kay

BITZRITZ, THE GOLDEN KRONE HOTEL
MRS. KATHERINE TELDON
HOLD EVERYTHING STOP I AM COMING STOP
TONY

ANTHONY'S DIARY

Two o'clock in the morning.

Marise and I must go back to the United States as soon as possible. Her sleepwalking is growing serious. I just had an awful fright.

I had just finished Dad's business when Kay's letter arrived. I left Buda-Pesth immediately. When I got off the train I stepped right into the special coach I had wired for. We drove up the mountains at top speed, but it seemed that the horses barely moved. The driver appeared to be in a hurry and he lashed them unmercifully.

We came to the foot of the last sharp rise and some part of the harness broke. We had to stop while the driver got out and fixed it. I hurried on afoot and soon neared "The Golden Krone." As my eyes became accustomed to the light I could make out the windows of our rooms. There is a small balcony off the largest one of them and I could see a white figure on it.

In a few moments I was near enough to recognize Marise.

I waved to her, thinking that perhaps Kay Teldon had told Marise I was coming and that she was waiting for me. There was no response, however, and I realized that she was lying half out of the window either in a faint or a deep sleep. I rushed up the stairs, woke the drowsy innkeeper, and hurried up to our rooms. I opened the door and found Risa's bed empty. Kay Teldon was lying in a deep slumber, breathing heavily.

After some trouble I woke Kay and, seeing that Risa was more than just asleep, we went across to the window. I lifted my wife and carried her back to her bed. She was very quiet and it seemed to me that she looked a trifle pale in the lamp-light. She must still have her cold for she was breathing through her parted lips and kept putting her hand to her throat as if it pained her. Kay apologized for being such a poor watcher and said it was the first time she had failed me. She could remember absolutely nothing after she and Risa had gone to bed. She recalled that her last drowsy thought was that the wolves were howling more loudly than usual, and then she again saw the huge bat at the window.

I certainly am going to take Risa home as soon as possible. She may love this country, but I don't. This last episode was a trifle too much. Somehow, this place is getting on my nerves.

Later

I spent all morning anxious. This condition can't continue. At noon the maid, or rather the innkeeper's daughter, called me. She said she had entered Madame's room and she was still asleep. To stay abed until noon here is an unpardonable crime and a sign of general laziness. Probably, as Marise had not rested the night before, she would sleep even later.

I noticed that after sunrise, Marise never had the slightest uneasiness. Because of this I had no compunctions about riding down with the innkeeper's son to get the mail, and, incidentally, to make arrangements for our return to the good old U.S.A.

When I got back, about four in the afternoon, the innkeeper's daughter informed me in a most reproachful voice that "Madame sleeps still."

I decided that Risa wouldn't sleep that late no matter how tired she was. I also realized that the bed was situated so the sun would have awakened her by shining directly on her face an hour ago.

I dashed upstairs and entered the room, finding her sleeping quietly. I woke her, although it was rather hard to make her respond to me. I noticed again her extreme pallor. She said that she wasn't really asleep, but just so tired and drowsy and lethargic that it was too much effort to get out of bed. She made me promise to wake her the next time she slept so late.

ANTHONY'S DIARY
The next day

Marise slept well last night, and this morning we went on another picnic. Although her cheeks were perfectly white she seemed happier and more rested than she has been for a great while.

We got back to the inn tired but content. She will sleep well tonight.

ANTHONY'S DIARY

I think the picnic was a godsend to us all. Marise didn't walk in her sleep last night, but slept like a baby. I was the one who was rather wakeful.

Perhaps it was my Paris boyhood, but I have never conquered that continental dislike of sleeping with the windows all wide open. Risa carefully opened them as she retired and I just as carefully closed them. I sat looking over the steppes for an hour or more, watching the dark shadows I knew to be wolves, and following the wheeling flight of the bats around the window. I saw one big chap that must have been Kay T's pet. The rooms here are without the blessing of steam heat, and so I took my wakeful self to bed, deciding to leave the chilly world outside to the bats and the wolves. At least they have fur coats and I haven't.

These bad dreams must be contagious. Last night it was my turn to sleep heavily. I was tortured with all sorts of horrible imaginings. This morning Marise was hard to wake again. She looked excessively pale and seemed to have lost all her energy. She spoke again of the pain in her throat and head. It must be a return of her cold, as I noticed she wore a scarf around her neck.

She was very listless all day, but this evening she appeared to be more herself. All her usual vivacity returned, and she was totally set against going to bed, arguing that she was not in the least tired. When we did finally go to our rooms she did not want me to turn out the light, saying that the total dark frightened her. To please her I left a small light going.

We are wrapped in one of these heavy fogs again. It is so thick that the messengers can't see their way to the city. I think Risa is too weak to travel much, but a change away from here would help her greatly.

MARISE'S DIARY

I have seen her again! The gray lady of the castle, but here, outside my window. I woke in the night feeling feverish and ill. There seemed to be no cool spot on my pillow. As my head turned to the fresh night air I saw her face — oh, it seems it is quite impossible, but I knew I was awake! I could hear Tony's heavy breathing beside me, feel the touch of the linen under my cheek, and as I saw her, I dug my nails into my palms. The marks are there this morning, angry crescents. Her face seemed to hang there framed in the darkness. Now the eyes seemed malevolent, the unwavering gaze of an ocelot.

A dark shadow loomed beside the gray lady. Her eyes closed, her arms folded across her face like great wings. All was quiet but I felt the battle of two stern wills. It was as though the night was hushed, waiting for the outcome of this silent strife. My heart pounded wildly. Why? I felt involved, helpless, the prize for which these elementals clashed.

The gray lady's face, those ocelot eyes, turned away. The arms shuddered. I wept for her, defeated. The tears were salty on my lips and my sob woke Tony. He put his arm around me and at last I slept.

Why, then, do I feel so depressed? Perhaps — oh, so many things — the gypsy funeral, perhaps — at least I imagine that's what it was.

From the window today, I saw the gypsies who camp around the castle in a slow procession from there. On a wagon was a heavy wooden casket being carried — where, I wondered? Where do they leave their dead, these transients of the steppes? Probably some unhallowed spot, as they are considered outside the church. I tried to pray for the poor soul in the casket, but the words wouldn't come. Dear Lord, what is happening to me? Into what dark country do I wander?

ANTHONY'S DIARY Continued

Risa's condition is much worse. She was not able to get out of bed this morning. I am very upset, of course. There seems to be nothing the matter with her, just that she is very, very weak and that she has no energy. She is so pale and bloodless that she gives one the impression of transparency.

We received another invitation from the Count, but of course Risa and I couldn't accept and Bob doesn't like him anyway. I rather thought that Kay fancied him, but all she said today was, "He's a beast." She had no reason to offer, except that she simply didn't like him anymore. Isn't that like a woman? Calling a silly prejudice a hunch and refusing to go against it?

The driver at last managed to get through the fog and to the station. I spent very little time in Buda-Pesth this time. I merely engaged a Doctor Freinhietz to come back with me.

Thank Heaven, I have all the money I need to pay him. I wired Father and he sent word to stay as long as we needed and to engage the best medical attention possible. I had to stay here all night, and I am rather worried. I hope Kay will stay with Marise tonight. I hate to leave her alone.

I like this doctor very much. He is an elderly man, about fifty, I should say, with iron gray hair. He is stout and very dependable-looking. It eases my heart just to be around him. He has taken all these bothersome details off my hands and treats me very much as if I were the sick one.

More trouble. When we arrived I found that Bob had a toothache last night and had insisted on having his wife to himself. That, of course, left Marise alone. She was still asleep when we arrived. The doctor and I went up directly and found her in a state of coma.

When we revived her, she was very weak and pathetically glad to see us. She is so thin and pale it breaks my heart to see her. If it were possible I would say that she had lost ten pounds overnight. She didn't want anything to eat, but the doctor coaxed her. No one could resist him.

As she was sipping a cup of weak broth, the doctor took me outside the room and asked me if she had received some wound lately. I assured him that she had not hurt herself, to the best of my knowledge. He told me, then, that she was nearly dead from loss of blood. It is a mystery: she has not been wounded and the amount of blood that she has lost would have drenched the bed with scarlet. There was not a scratch on her except a very small cut on the throat.

Risa is in a very serious condition and the doctor assured me that a transfusion would be necessary to save her life. He asked my blood-type and was delighted to find it was O.

He is getting ready and will call for me at any moment. He has given her a hypodermic. I must admit I'm frightened and, to say the least, puzzled.

CHAPTER NINE

ANTHONY'S DIARY Continued

I am writing this as I lie on the porch of the inn. I am now feeling as weak and listless as Risa did such a short while ago. It was a dreadful experience, feeling your life blood being drained from your veins, but just to see the rosy color stealing back into Risa's pale cheeks and to see my darling lose that dreadful look made it all worthwhile. She confessed that she had walked in her sleep last night. It is odd that she should always go out on the balcony.

Risa is sleeping now. Poor dear, she has been robbed of rest for so many nights. She said the sunlight made her drowsy. She has slept all afternoon and, now, as the sun is setting, she is calling for me.

MARISE'S DIARY

These awful experiences of the last few days are weighing on me dreadfully. This morning I was feeling so weak and spiritless I thought I would never have the strength to open my eyes.

I was so glad to see Tony and that dear doctor he brought with him. I felt as if some haunting presence had been removed from me. I was so afraid to face another night alone. The only blot on my happiness is this: Tony and the doctor insist on treating me as a baby. I know something serious is the matter, and yet they won't tell me the trouble. The doctor examined me and then took Tony out into the corridor. A few minutes later they came back, Tony told me to be a good girl and that the doctor was going to give me something to put me to sleep. When I woke up it was late in the afternoon. The nap rested me wonderfully. I feel like a new woman. The color has returned to my cheeks and I feel alive once more. I immediately called for Tony. The poor boy has been so worried, and I knew he'd be relieved to see me looking so much better. But the doctor said, "Let him rest. He's tired from his journey."

I heard him add, though... "brave lad..."

Poor, poor Tony. He is as white as a sheet. He has been worried over me and has not slept. His trip to Buda-Pesth tired him. I can see that clearly. He is as pale as I was this morning.

ANTHONY'S DIARY

Both of us were very tired this night and went to bed early. Risa's looking so much better this evening that I think we'll be able to get home within a week. I have telegraphed home again. Dad cabled to have me let him know how she was every day.

The doctor is going to stay here at "The Golden Krone" as long as there is the slightest danger. He has also written to Buda-Pesth for his friend and associate, Doctor Kurn. He was not satisfied with what he found concerning my wife's condition, and wanted Kurn for a consultation.

Continued

Risa was so much better after her good night's sleep. Both Kay and Bob were in to see her and she was quite herself again. I am fine this morning, too. In this bright sunlight all our fears and forebodings of last night seem futile and far away. There is no tonic like this blessed sun. Both Risa and I are reveling in it. After all the fog and darkness it is like a cheery benediction.

Last night after Risa had gone to bed, the Count called to ask after her. At first I wondered how he knew she was ill, but I realized that in these small villages such news travels fast. He was "very unhappy to hear that the most charming lady was indisposed."

I don't know whether I like that fellow. I think I could be fond of him if he would let me. He impresses me as being a very lonely fellow. It must be ghastly to live up there in that half-ruined dump alone, with none of his own class for miles around. He is so standoffish and formal. I'd be willing to bet six bits (and I didn't get all "A's" in Psychology in college for nothing) that he has what Freud would call an inferiority complex. The more I look at that last sentence the more "Kay Teldon-ish" it appears. But, them's my sentiments.

I asked the Count in, as it was so cold out last night, and at first he looked surprised, then satisfied, then ashamed, or so it seemed. He thanked me but declined my invitation, bid me an abrupt good night, and galloped off.

Everything is so peaceful and natural now. Marise is sleeping in the sun, Bob and Kay are scrapping in the inn, and I am lazily scribbling in my notebook. It is too good to be true.

Continued

Some dismal spirit of prophecy must have prompted me to write those last words. Last night I slept heavily and this morning when I woke, Risa was as before. She was lying on the bed, dead white with her mouth open, and the pale lips shrunken back over her teeth. I called the Doctor immediately. He stood for a moment gazing at her with the pained and baffled expression of an adoring dog, whose master has whipped him without cause. Then he gave a low cry as he sank on his knees beside the bed. In a moment he recovered himself and rolled up his sleeves. He put Risa in a hot bath and made ready for another transfusion. No hypo was needed this time, as my poor darling was past all pain. The thing that puzzled me, and that I noticed even as I realized her condition, was that there was no blood on the bed and none on her clothes except for a small drop on the pillow.

The Doctor gave Risa another transfusion. When she revived, a short while after the transfusion, she was so pale and weak that she could not stand. I feel as I did after the fever in South America. The doctor says that I cannot stand another donation transfusion. I do not know what we will do if this condition occurs again. I am merely writing this down as a duty. If I did not make it a practice to enter each happening in my Diary I don't think I would have opened it for the last week.

My wife asked for her journal, too. It frightened me. She seemed to have something on her mind that she wanted to put down. I do not know why I like to write those words, "My wife," unless it is that I am afraid that — but I must not think of such things.

NOTES OF DOCTOR FRIENHEITZ

I have never found myself in such a case as this, my present one. The poor woman is dying for lack of blood. Her brave husband will die if I take any more from him. There is no sign of a wound, except for that small mark on her throat. (Note: watch that mark. It is not healing properly.) And after each transfusion she is soon in as bad need as ever. (Note: why is there no blood stain after such bleeding?) I feel I must save her — not only for professional reasons, but for the husband and for herself and last of all for one foolish, old German doctor. I must go now, for they inform me that my friend Kurn has arrived. Maybe he will find the source of all this trouble.

Later

There will be no matter now of finding someone who will give blood for the dear Madame Risa. The American friend Bob Teldon came to me and said,

"Doctor, if there is any way that I can help with these transfusions, I mean, please let me. I'm a type O, too. Tony has told me. You see, Tony and I went to college together, and we all grew up together. I was once in love with Marise myself, and Tony and Kay — oh, I know that this all sounds awfully mixed up, but you see that we are all very close to one another. We would do anything for Risa."

Even more now I am liking these young Americans.

KAY TELDON'S JOURNAL

This all so dreadful about poor Risa. Both Bob and I are doing all that we can, but I think I feel the worst for poor Tony. It must be perfectly horrible to see one's wife dying by inches. If only the doctors could find what is wrong. And if only Tony would get her out of this

God-forsaken hole. I feel she would be so much safer.

Bob offered some of his blood for the transfusion this evening. I did, too, but I don't have the right type. I'm glad. I think I'd pass out in the process.

The Count was here again this evening. I hate him. I wish he would keep that pale face of his out of here. Always snooping around. That awful pallor and those cold eyes just give me the creeps. I was sitting in the room here sewing, they had just lighted the lamps, as the sunset was fading rapidly. I don't know what it was that made me turn around, but there he was. He had a perfect right to come into the lobby of the inn if he wanted to, but he needn't go pussyfooting about like that. I was startled and I told him so. All he said was,

"My foot is light."

Too darned light, if you ask me.

Oh how I hate this place. We would leave, but Tony says Risa is too weak to travel, and both Bob and I agree that we ought to be near, in case something should happen.

What is the matter with me? I never used to break down this way... Darned Fool!

ANTHONY'S DIARY

Three days later.

Risa is sinking swiftly... I cannot bear to go on. The doctors hold no hope for her. I have wired Dad, although there was no special good in that. He can do nothing for either of us.

She sleeps all day long. Only at night does she rouse herself. I have not even bothered to go to bed for the last few nights, I know I cannot sleep. I would rather be awake and beside her, in case she should call me.

There have been no more transfusions, as the doctors say there will be no reason for me to weaken myself, when I will soon be needing my strength, the inference is.

Oh, Marise...

Later

Marise rose tonight in her sleep. She who has been too feeble to raise her head, got up out of her bed and walked. They speak of the strength of the mad — not, of course, that Risa is out of her head — but I feel that the strength she shows while she is walking in her sleep is in some way related to that other power. She is certainly not herself. She walked across the room and lifted a pillow on the couch. At first I tried to get her back in bed, but then I waited and watched her.

She took out a small book which I knew was her diary. She has often asked for it these last few days, hoarding her strength to make the entries. She always seems to feel better after her writing. Once I asked her what she entered, now that she was not doing anything. She did not answer, but said evasively, "You may know someday. God knows, I don't understand what I put down. Dreams. Read it after..."

To my great surprise, she took the book firmly in her poor weak hands and tried to rip it across. The cover gave at the binding, and I could see that the diary she had so carefully guarded would soon be scraps of paper. I gently took it from her hands. She continued the tearing motion, and then at last she opened her hands and made a gesture as if to scatter the pieces of torn diary. After that she went back to bed. A few minutes later she awoke and seemed surprised to see me. She complained that her throat hurt, and I went in search of Doctor Frienheitz.

I am going to read her diary. It is a thing I would never do if she were herself, but I feel that perhaps this little volume may hold the secret of her malady. She said it contained her dreams. If these dreams are the functioning of her subconscious mind, as the scientists say they are, they may be a clue to her illness. Might they not be her impressions, her suspicions that she does not wish to tell us? I think if Risa were herself she would want me to read this book.

I have read Marise's Diary. My God! Can it be delirium, or can it be... true?

CHAPTER TEN

MARISE'S DIARY

Again those fearful dreams. Last night while I was sleeping I half awoke with the realization that someone was calling to me. Still asleep and yet awake, I went out on the balcony. The bats were so close, the air full of fog. A sensation of great weariness came over me and I fell to the floor.

There was one great burning star above my head. Languidly I watched it, watched it as it doubled and two stars gazed at me like burning eyes. I saw the mist disappearing, vanishing, and, as it went, I saw a tall figure bending down to me. Strong arms lifted me tenderly, and as the moon rose from its blanket of clouds I could make out the features of the Count. I was not afraid, I was too weary to even question his presence on my balcony.

I forgot everything — Tony, my life, all. Just one thing remained in the present. He was there, and I was in his arms. I saw his dark, handsome face bending down over me. I swayed forward, reluctant, yet I was as powerless as a tall tree driven by the wind. I knew he was going to kiss me and — I must put it down, although some day it may hurt Tony to read this — I did not wish to prevent him. I forgot everything, in his arms.

And then for centuries I was deep in still waters. All was at peace. Then pain, sharp as the flash of sunlight on blue steel... and then, Oblivion.

When, after aeons I came back, I seemed to be floating on a dark sea. The water was lapping somewhere far away on a distant shore, or it might only have been my breathing. It was all so quiet, the water was washing against my face. I knew that soon the water would cover me, and that would be the end. I did not mind, I was so tired.

Then, somewhere, someone was calling someone. The water ceased to lap so near my lip. I sighed, I wanted rest.

Somewhere... calling. The dark sea was vanishing into mist. Ever that calling. Just one word over and over again. It had meant something to me once, long ago. I struggled to remember.

I felt other arms lifting me, not as strong as His. There was a jerk, and I remembered. Tony was leaning over me, as He had. I was so glad to be back again, with Tony. I had voyaged far over the Dark Sea.

This is my Dream as I remember it. I hope that someday Tony will read it, and if possible, understand.

MARISE'S DIARY
Two days later

Again those dreams. Again He was here. This time He came into the room, I looked at Tony. He was so sound asleep. I could not wake him. He spoke to me.

"I want you. Come to me."

I rose from the bed and walked across the room. I was not so weak as before. Somehow his very presence had given me strength. I looked at Tony. He read the question in my eyes. He laughed.

"You would hesitate because of him? Do not be a fool. He is but a mortal. I am offering you Life! Life forever. We shall watch dynasties rise and fall. Together. See the nations of the earth lead, or crumble into dust. Together.

"Would you live a petty score or so of years? — or live with me for centuries? This am I offering you: my name, my castle, and... LIFE!..." His voice had sunk to a sibilant whisper... "Marise, Marise, will you come?"

My answer burst from my lips. He wanted me, and I must go.

"You are Master. I will do as you wish."

He stepped near to me, and then he took me in his arms. Again and again He kissed me. He seemed to draw all power of resistance out of me. I lay there, motionless, and powerless. Even in the darkness His eyes seemed to burn into me with an unearthly radiance. I was content. He was Master. Ever my thoughts reverted to His promise.

"How," I whispered, "how?"

"Our Mystic Sacrament," He answered. And as He spoke He parted the collar of the soft dark shirt that He wore. With one of His long, sharp nails He opened a vein at the base of His throat. As the blood sprang forth He pressed my lips against it. There was an acrid, salty taste in my mouth, and I fainted.

This morning I awoke on my bed, as weak as ever, and yet with a feeling of unreality, because of my dream. I have decided to destroy this Diary. It is dangerous. I would like to keep it, but an order came from the Master. I must obey. A force and a will outside my own is commanding me. Tonight I shall do as He wishes.

ANTHONY'S DIARY

I dare not, cannot, believe that which Risa has written. It is all impossible. And yet, that book of Abbe Calmet's spoke of such things as this. It is all some dreadful nightmare, too preposterous to believe. I do not know why, but I do not wish to show this to the Doctor. I will keep it and maybe someday I will be able to solve this riddle.

It is a dismal night. The fire is burning low and the bats are flapping most angrily at the windows. I have just been in to see Risa and she is sleeping. It is odd that she should sleep so much. She is not beautiful tonight. Her lips are parted and her breathing is labored. Her teeth are even and white, but are too much in evidence. Her mouth is ravenous with the long eye teeth denting her lip. The gums are shrunken and her lips are parched. I would think she had a fever, but she is so pale. She's dying, and I must stand here, helpless.

It is almost dawn — that hour when the world seems to stand poised between dark and light, undecided. Marise is calling me.

Later

Marise has made me promise something. When I entered her room she was lying awake, watching for me. I knelt down beside her, and she laid her hands in mine.

"Tony," she said, "I want you make me a vow, that if I should die, you will bury me here in the land I have loved. Will you do that? And, Tony, kiss me good-bye now. Kiss me just once and go. There. Oh, Tony, Tony... dear... good-bye."

I stumbled out of the room, half blinded by my tears. I promised, and I will keep my vow.

After that I do not remember. I know I ran out of the inn and up the mountain. I know that for hours I climbed, and that at last I fell exhausted at the summit. I returned to the inn in the late afternoon, when the long molten rays of the setting sun gleamed softly, like a benediction on all mankind. Alas, for me there is no peace. All my hopes and dreams are soon to be buried with my dear Risa.

Dusk... the Doctor is calling me.

The little room where Marise lay was dim. The night was falling over the inn in the Carpathians. The white bed gleamed eerily through the murkiness. There was a silence that brooded over the place. Beside the window, Kay Teldon was crying softly. Her husband stood beside her, patting her heaving shoulder mechanically, his eyes on the still, white figure in the bed. The doctor laid his hands upon Tony's shoulder. Tony understood as clearly as if he had spoken. No need for words. She was dying. He moved forward and knelt beside her.

The fire flared and threw Marise's white face into a Rembrandt-like relief against the shadowy background. Her eyes were open, and their darkness was startling contrast to the pallor of her face. Her lids, which half hid her eyes, were like the waxen black-purple color that one sometimes sees at the base of a poppy petal. Although her cheeks were almost colorless, her lips were moist and scarlet, half parted, showing her small white teeth. Her dark hair lay in two thick braids against the pillow. Her faltering breath scarcely stirred the sheet, and her tall, slender body made hardly a ridge in the coverings.

Marise's eyes seemed fixed on the window, watching the sunset. As the twilight thickened she turned to Tony. As she spoke, her voice drew them all to her side with its strangeness.

Gone was the husky contralto, and in its place was a voluptuous sweetness, a clear, metallic quality.

"Tony? Tony, where are you?"

"Here, Risa, right here, darling."

"Kiss me... good-bye..."

As Anthony leaned forward eagerly, Kay Teldon grasped his arm and screamed as she pointed,

"Look, look, a bat... at the window!"

In the silence that followed, Marise gave a gasping sigh, half rose from the bed, and then fell back. She was dead.

After a long moment, Tony lifted his head from his hands and said, "She didn't have a chance, Kay, to kiss me... to kiss me good-bye..."

Cablegram from Anthony Morrow to Mr. Durant Morrow

MR. DURANT MORROW
10 MALBROUGH PLACE
BOSTON MASS
RISA DIED AT FIVE THIRTY STOP MALADY UNKNOWN STOP PROCEEDING TO LONDON STOP WIRE FURTHER INSTRUCTIONS THERE STOP WILL STAY WITH HARKERS STOP TONY

ANTHONY'S DIARY

I have kept my promise to Risa. She was buried at the little church at Bitzritz. I am leaving this land that is so full of dreadful memories. I came here, full of hope and love, and now I leave, broken, with the dearest things gone out of my life. The Teldons are returning to New York immediately. I can never thank them for all their sympathy and kindness.

Poor Doctor Frienheitz was all broken up over Marise's death. He seemed to think it was all his fault, yet I know he did all possible to save her. He and Doctor Kurn are going as far as Buda-Pesth with me.

I cannot bear to think of leaving my darling here all alone, but now she does not need me. Life stretches before me, a long and lonely road. The way will be hard without her. That which was so full of hope and promise is empty now, and bitter with disillusionment.

The diligence is ready now, and I am leaving "The Golden Krone" forever. Good-bye, Transylvania. Good-bye, love. Good-bye... Marise.

93

CHAPTER ELEVEN

A fog was drifting in over the Baltic, a white blanket that covered plains and hills and, growing bolder, carried its inexorable march up the mountain, feeling with opaque fingers for a foothold in the crevasses. It swallowed all that stood in its way, overwhelmed a peasant's hut, and changed a tall pine into a ghost that moaned with the voice of the wind.

It even dared to rise to the heavens and blot out the stars, and drown the moon in a misty sea. Upward and upward it carried its march, until the village of Bitzritz was engulfed in a tidal wave of woolly whiteness, and the oblong windows of "The Golden Krone" were mere fuzzy glow worms that clung crazily to a murky wall.

The fog had reached the castle on the top of the hill. It wove through the tattered battlements and wrapped the crumbling towers in its folds. The little churchyard brooded under its milky pall. Tombstones gleamed faintly through the fog.

In a corner, under the funereal shade of a mountain ash, stood a small tomb of white marble. The tree trailed its long branches across the tomb and stenciled its veined walls as the half light filtered through its bare and tangled branches. The wind crooned a chromatic, monotonous lullaby, and rattled as if knocking. The tomb stood lonely and apart from the other graves. Against the door crumbled decaying flowers, the melancholy russets and grays making a somber stain against the whiteness.

Out of the night and the mist a bat came flying. It circled the graveyard once or twice, and at last came to rest in the mountain ash.

Inside the tomb rested a casket. Its dark sides were draped with a faded garland that exuded a soft perfume of roses and lilies. The moonlight came faintly through a grating in the ceiling, barely illuminating the interior and making pale splotches on the floor.

Tiny grains of dust were whirling in a fantastic dance, sliding down the moonbeams, only to be wafted into the air again. Their aerial gamboling became swifter and swifter, gathering together in a nebulous way — not singly, but in groups. Faster, thicker. At last they seemed to take on a dim phantom shape. A figure appeared in the beam. It was but a matter of seconds before it materialized and a dark shape bent over the casket. Hands fumbled at the catch and then at last threw back the lid. Inside, a shape gleamed faintly white in the darkness. A sharp metallic whisper cut through the silence,

"Marise, Marise..."

Down... Down... Down... For centuries she was sinking through cool green water. There was an intolerable ringing in her ears. Suffocation and weariness. A dazzling flash of light cut across her eyeballs. She opened her eyes to see Tony leaning over her, his haggard face lighted by the setting sun.

"Tony, Tony..." she called to him. Tony would come, too, if she could kiss him... Oblivion, and the Pain.

So for days she lay. She was dead to all appearances; as a mortal, dead. She did not change, except that the expression was not that which she had worn, and the sweet eyes were closed, never to open again with the pure and happy light that had smiled in their depths. She lay as she had that evening when she... died.

Out of the darkness came light. Out of the silence, a voice. It was calling her name. Strong arms about her, lifting her, and then she remembered. She struggled back to consciousness and gently disengaged herself from his embrace. She laughed, clearly, like the tinkling of glass. She stood before him, tall and beautiful, bridelike in her white robes. She seemed an angel, with her dark hair soft about her and her hands clasped against her bosom. An angel, all but her face. Her long lashes half veiled her eyes, and the full red lips were parted, inviting.

Marise moved forward, her gown rustling as she went. She twined her arms about him and let her fingers wander across his cheek and hide themselves in his dark hair. Tall as she was she could hear his heart beating wildly as she laid her head on the dark cloak that covered it.

"You did love me," she said, "your heart is telling me so. Oh, beloved, you are so strong, you are killing me, I cannot breathe..."

He swept her into his arms, bending her backwards, breaking down all resistance under the tempest of his caresses. He kissed her lips, her eyes, and her throat, leaving her quiet and passive in his arms.

"My darling," he whispered, his lips against her hair, "you were worth waiting for, all the centuries, and now you are mine for all the Ages to come."

Gathering her limp form into his arms he carried her across the small room of the tomb to the door and, still holding her, passed through.

He soon returned and stood before the casket. He grasped the handle and pulled with all his great strength. It gave before him, even though it was sealed. Carefully he reclosed it and turned again into the darkness.

Up at the castle Marise stood looking from the window of "her room". It was the same one in which she had first seen the man who was to change the whole course of her life. She turned quickly, with a smile of welcome, as he appeared in the doorway.

"Come with me," he called.

Together they descended the steep, wide stairs and, passing through the great hall, they disappeared down one of the yawning passageways. Down even further they went, descending a spiral staircase and stopping at last in front a heavy door. This he opened, revealing an almost subterranean chapel room.

The small mullioned windows were paned with a heavy, yellowish glass that threw a lurid glare over the piles of dust and the crumbling masonry. Here and there, mounted on small daises were heavy stone tombs, all engraved with the Dracula arms. Others were set in niches, with short flights of steps leading up to them. At one end was a chantry altar, beautifully carved and decorated but with the tabernacle empty. Marise drew forward with a little cry of pleasure at seeing it.

"You like the altar?" he asked. "It is Italian, work of the sixteenth century. I bought it from a man from Florence. It is sadly out of repair."

"Even so," she answered, "I think it is perfect. Time has softened the colors and the tracery is like frozen lace. This whole chapel is like that."

Under a high window was a small platform that was empty. The Count contemplated it for a moment and then made a gesture of resolution. Turning to Marise, who was busy reading the inscription on a casket of evident antiquity, he said,

"Come, dear one. It is growing late, and we have work to do before dawn."

In spite of the fog, the gypsies were making merry that night. Their campfires gleamed weirdly in the mist, throwing long elastic shadows and lighting the dark glen. The musicians had taken out their violins and their guitars, making ready for the dancers. Small laughing groups gathered in the pool of light, anticipating the evening's entertainment. Already a score of voices were singing one of those hauntingly plaintive songs that characterize gypsy music the world over.

These bands of gypsy vagabonds that roved over all Hungary are as familiar as the trees and the steppes. They usually attach themselves to some lord or noble, and spend the winter months under his care, or at least, his protection. Thus, for centuries, the Zigany served the Draculas, passing the severe winters under the shadow of the castle wall, and feeding their herds on the rolling plains. A lazy, fierce band of people, as loyal to their patron lord as the knights of feudalism were to their liege.

So it was, that cold fall night, that the "hetman," or chief, of the Zigany felt a hand upon his shoulder and, turning, saw his master standing in the moonlight, just outside of the radiance thrown by the leaping flames.

"There is work to be done," the Count told the chief in a low voice. "Bring six men and come with me."

Bowing low, the "hetman" turned and went towards one of the laughing groups around the fire. He soon returned, followed by six stalwart young gypsies, ready for anything their lord should command. Silently they passed through the fog and the night until they came to the little church graveyard at Bitzritz. There on the outskirts of the yard, they hesitated as the Count gave them his orders. Silently, they disappeared into the gloom and soon reappeared, carrying a long, dark object with them.

CHAPTER TWELVE

Through the tightly closed doors of the inn came sounds of great revelry. The musicians' busy fingers plied the bow or plucked the strings industriously. The busy innkeeper and his wife bustled here and there with foaming steins of golden ale and huge trays of small, sweet cakes. All the townsfolk had come to the inn for dancing and feasting, for it was truly said, "Foul weather without is fair weather within."

Mara, the innkeeper's black-eyed daughter, was even more preoccupied than her father and sisters, for Nikolas, the goat-herder was there. Even though her father frowned on his ardent suit and she coyly pretended that she didn't even see him, Nikolas knew that he was being slyly watched out of eyes black as sloes, and he knew it was his presence that brought that blush to Mara's cheeks. Often in the lively spirals of the dances Nikolas would press Mara's hand and beg for a moment to speak with her. Finally she consented, and they disappeared onto the dark porch where Tony and Marise had spent so many happy hours together, before the new, strange life had begun for Marise.

"Mara, my angel," he whispered, "I would do anything to prove my love for you. Won't you believe me?"

She laughed as she pressed her hand over his mouth.

"You know, Nikolas, if I thought you would speak of things like this, I would not have come. Let us talk of — talk of the meinherr American and his lovely wife. Was she not beautiful?"

"Beautiful," he agreed absently, much to Mara's surprise, for that was not the response that she had expected.

"Oh," she continued, "and wasn't her death so sad? Do you know what I think?..." She stopped herself quickly.

Nikolas glanced up hurriedly and, reading her thought in her eyes, he nodded solemnly as they both crossed themselves and made the sign to ward off the evil eye.

Mara rose to her feet and said, hesitantly, "L-l-let us go in, Nikolas. I-I do not like it out here now. It is so dark, and I am frightened."

"Don't be frightened, dear. I am here. You know I would never let anything harm you. I feel as strong as a lion when you are by my side."

She slipped out of his enfolding arms and called back tauntingly from the door, "If you are so brave, Master Lion, why don't you go look and see if she is in there? You know what I mean. Perhaps if you find out, I might, only might, listen to what you have to say!"

"Mara," he called. "Do you really mean it? Do you?"

"Didn't I say it?" she answered with the woman's delight in teasing the one she loves.

"Then, by all the Saints, I will go," he declared — and before she could stop him, Nickolas was off and down the steps. Mara went back to the inn and carefully closed the door. She watched by the window, peering out into the darkness with anxious eyes.

Through the night Nikolas walked bravely. He wished, however, that the moon would rise and peep through the clouds, or that the mist would roll away. The light of the inn seemed small and distant as he trudged onward. An owl in a crumbling tree plaintively inquired, "Whooo? Whoooo?"

The very sound of the wind seemed to increase Nikolas' loneliness. He wished that he had called his dog. Once he was on the point of turning back, but he tossed his head, threw back his shoulders, and marched resolutely on.

It was worth it to him, whatever the price. If only Mara would let him convince her that he loved her! This mission in the night, if anything, would prove his devotion. Resolutely, he tried to keep his thoughts on the pleasures to come and not on the dreadful possibilities that lay before him.

There is nothing in human life or within the range of human knowledge that is as terrifying as The Unknown. It is the uncertainty of the dark that makes little children fear to be left alone without a light. It is the reason that men fear Death.

Nikolas did not know where he was going nor what he would find when he reached there. He was helpless. He was marching against an enemy and he had no weapons. Little would his physical strength avail him if — he quickly brushed the thought from his mind. Running through his tortured brain were all the folklore and the traditions of his race. Again and again he thought of the strange tales that his mother and grandmother had told him, tales handed down through the generations, of the great school at Scholomance, hid in the mountains over Lake Hermanistadt, where all the arts of Darkness were taught, and where the Devil claimed every tenth student as his due. There, it was said that the "stregoica," or witches, of old had learned their magic arts, among them the secret of eternal life.

Soon Nikolas could make out the church in the ebbing mist. Pushing aside the sagging gate, he entered the graveyard. Trembling, he made his way to the little tomb in the corner. With a last desperate spurt he reached the door of the tomb, threw it open in a frenzy of courage and fear, and gazed within. Then he pushed the door closed and left as fast as his legs would carry him.

For the thousandth time, Mara peered from the window of the inn, thinking for the ten thousandth time that she saw Nikolas coming.

"If I have sent him to his death I shall die, too," she wailed, as she turned away.

Then through the night and fog she saw him at last. He was disheveled and tired with running. He threw himself upon the porch and panted and rested his heavy head in his hands.

"She was not... there. Even the coffin was gone!" he told Mara in a stifled voice.

"Then she —" Mara could not finish. "Oh, my darling, to think I sent you into that awful place." And Mara sank down beside Nikolas on the step, thankful that no dark cloud hovered in the sky of their happiness and threatened to blot out the sunshine of their hopes.

CHAPTER THIRTEEN

ANTHONY'S DIARY
Vienna

At last I am getting out of this awful land. Although I can never forget her, already the memories of those last terrible hours are becoming a dream that I have half forgotten, with only a hazy impression of horror that taunts me.

I am very thankful that within a few weeks I shall be in London with the Harkers. I know I can rest there. I dread the day when I shall have to return to America and answer all those thousands of sympathetic questions and give all the morbid details. The kindest thing my family can do, under these circumstances, is to leave me alone.

Everywhere I go, the people have been the embodiment of kindness. For the last week I have stayed with the kind Doctor Frienheitz and his wife. I left him at Buda-Pesth, however.

I have been quite fortunate in making arrangements on the boat and train to have a cabin and compartment all to myself. I decided the trip to England by sea would do me more good than the same journey by land.

I have arranged for young Quincy Harker to meet me at Bristol. It seems odd to write "young Harker," for he is only a year or so younger than I am. I haven't seen him for years. The last time, I believe, was in Paris. We went to the same art school there several years ago. That family is as much addicted to globe-trotting as I am. It was Mr. Harker that influenced Risa and I to go to the Balkans. Harker senior has built up quite a large clientele these last years. He is a "barrister," I believe.

I am going to stay with them at their London place for a week or so, just long enough to finish up some work for Dad. Quincy's mother died last year, so they have given up their large home and are living quite simply, to judge from Quin's somewhat intermittent letters.

I have always wished I could have known Mrs. Harker better. I have heard that she was quite an interesting person, and from what I learned from Quincy, she had a full and eventful life. But I shall never hear her tales, now.

Later

I'm absolutely bored stiff. There's not a thing to do aboard this ship. I would almost welcome a storm by way of diversion, and from the looks of the sky, we might be in for some fun, if you choose to call it that.

This is not one of those large, palatial ocean liners, all fitted up for deck tennis, with a bathing pool and a miniature golf course.

I wired the Harkers that I would be coming and they answered that Quin would be waiting for me. It seems he's staying with friends at Bath. He assured me it would not be at all out of his way to welcome me to England in person.

I only remember him faintly. We must have been about fifteen or sixteen when we last saw each other. That was ten years ago. We've kept up a rather sketchy correspondence, only writing when the spirit moved us. I haven't heard from him since last year, when he wrote of his mother's death. She was a wonderful lady, to hear Quin's tales of her courage and adventuresome spirit. I expect all her stories have perished with her.

The Teldons left the same time I did, poor Kay fairly loaded down with the miles of peasant embroidery Risa had bought. I gave it all to her, together with the pottery. I could not bear to have them around.

It is surprising what a host of memories one small object will call up. This morning I found a hairpin inside the tray of my trunk and, for a moment, it seemed the world was a little sunnier and that there was no such thing as death... Then I remembered.

ANTHONY'S DIARY
Later

We have run into some dirty weather, and all the passengers have been told to stay below the decks. I suppose the smells of a sailing vessel are the sweetest perfumes in the world to some people, but I certainly can't recognize their charm. Down in my cabin one can get unmistakable whiffs of all that's cooked in the galley, an experience not very comforting to one who is the slightest bit seasick. Thank Heaven, I've always been immune to that bugaboo of sea travel. All the aroma of tar and bilge water wafts through my porthole. Only a hardened seaman can stand this stifling atmosphere!

Even so, I am enjoying my journey, trying to forget. We have quite a trip ahead of us. In spite of this recent below-deck confinement, the fresh air each day, all day long, has done me a world of good.

Later

The storm has passed and we are now in a lull. There's scarcely any wind, and all the sails are flapping idly. We are allowed to go up on the deck again, and I tell you, the fresh air is wonderful!

I certainly wish I could find some magazines that are less than four months old, which ripe old age most of these on board have reached.

I have learned from the other "prisoners" that one of them is a wealthy stockman from Australia, who stopped off on the continent for awhile and is now bound for the good, old

"Hisland 'ome." Another is a missionary, and another, an ex-army officer who has spent most of his life in India and who is so shy that most of his vocabulary consists of "I say!"

There is an elderly American woman on a self-conducted tour, very determined to see all there is to see in this world; and a couple of English girls out with their aunt. The aunt is the perfect personification of the lady in the Gilbert-Sullivan opera who "doesn't think she waltzes but would rather like to try." I know because I have tried it.

My only consolation is my diary. Even it lies to me. That which I have just written, for instance, I don't mean it. I am afraid to admit even to myself how terrible I really feel. I like to pretend I am cheerful and so I enter these kind of things in my little book.

I almost threw my diary overboard the other day. I opened it to one of the back pages and read one of the entries I had made in it before Marise... left. I am trying to forget, but no matter what I do, she seems so close to me. I feel we will always be together. I cannot think of her as dead. Her image is always before me. I keep seeing her as I saw her last, the day she was buried. She didn't seem dead, but sleeping. There was not that blankness of expression that characterizes the dead, but, rather, animation, as though she was merely quiet for the moment. I know we shall meet again. Fool that I am!

ANTHONY'S DIARY
Later

Another dreary day has dragged by. This same routine of getting up, dressing, going to the officers' mess to get my breakfast, killing time until noon, lunch, more time passing, dinner, writing, and smoking until it is bedtime is terrible! Last year I used to weep and wail because I had so many things to do and no time in which to attend to them all. Now I am absolutely bored.

I have heard from the Teldons only once since they went home. I think, after all, I shall be glad to get home. I'll have my work to occupy my mind, and then I can forget... perhaps.

I used to love the sea but now it is as dreary and as unending as my own thoughts. It is the same monotonous round, over and over. I feel rather sorry for the ocean. It's been doing the same thing for centuries, and I have all my life stretching out before me, as lonely and as gray as these waters. I must not be morbid, though, and I should remember that the sea is not always stormy, and that the sunshine has always appeared after the rain. But how can there be sunshine if the sun has dropped from the sky?

The next day

We are arriving in Bristol today. Oh, blessed activity! I've packed and repacked my trunk, looked over my different papers that will be necessary to present on landing, searched the cabin for the inevitable leftovers, and am getting all in order for the landing.

CHAPTER FOURTEEN

Tony pressed eagerly down through the swarming crowds of dock men and sailors from ships that lined the harbor, in search of his friend. At the other end of the wharf, Quincy Harker stood on the running board of his car and gazed over the heads of the milling mob around him. Soon their eyes met, and, in but a moment, the two friends were reunited. Their warm handclasp spoke volumes. No need for words. All the sympathy and pity in the world glowed in the steady gray-blue eyes of the younger man.

In a flash Quincy and Tony both had regained their customary poise.

"Tony, old man," Quincy gasped, "awfully glad to see you."

"Golly, Quin," Tony returned warmly, "you haven't changed a bit."

"Of course not. I told you I hadn't. But we'd better be going. We have quite a distance before us."

As the little car purred its way up and over the winding road to London, old intimacy was renewed, and each found in each other the same qualities they had admired in their youth. The old affection welled up a hundredfold with a sudden realization that this was a friendship that would survive the passing of years.

For awhile, there was the usual light chatter of those who are merely talking to make conversation, the rather restrained manner of semi-strangers, but this soon gave way to recollections, summoned by the sight of familiar faces and surroundings. Finally they lapsed into complete silence as the little gray car sped into the deepening dusk.

To Tony, the familiar English countryside called up many happy memories of the happy years of his boyhood and the days he had attended school on the continent. In the soft gloaming, he felt a sudden sting in his eyes, a pang of nostalgia.

"You know, Quin," Tony said, "I can't get used to this crossing of the country in one day or so. I'm used to my blessed U.S. where it's miles and miles across one state."

There was no answer to his remark. The silence fell again. The fog that was creeping from the sea, coupled with the mysterious twilight, brought back many poignant memories of the honeymoon. Tony tried to imagine Marise here by his side, her face bright in the semidarkness.

After a time, Quincy turned his gaze from the hazy road and said,
"I suppose you don't have any fog in your 'blessed U.S.' If that is so, I'm afraid you're in for a spell of it here in London!"

"Oh, no," Tony returned. "I'm quite used to it; I've just come from the Balkans, you know."

Then for a time neither man spoke. The car headlights pried ahead into the murky road with golden fingers. The wheels made small hissing sounds as they sped over the glistening asphalt. Now and then they passed small wayside houses with their lighted windows, but for the most part they were entirely alone on the moor. The salty wind ruffled their hair with soft caresses or brushed their faces with moist fingers. Onward and onward they rolled, past fences and trees blurredly silhouetted against the silvery sky. All had a faint air of unreality in the gloom. The powerful motor hummed a little song to itself contentedly.

Finally they stopped at a small tavern for food. As they turned into the small courtyard with its mossy flagstone, Anthony was reminded of "The Golden Krone." It seemed as though the whole country was conspiring to make him remember those painful incidents he was trying so hard to forget.

Inside they welcomed the cheery blaze of the hooded fireplace with the tempting kettle on a crane that hung beside it. For the first time since leaving the ship, Tony realized how ravenously hungry he was. When the tavernkeeper brought foaming steins of ale and the remainder of a tasty pigeon pie, he attacked them with a good will.

"We ought to reach London by midnight, at least," said Quincy as they climbed back in the car.

"Don't hurry on my account," begged Tony, "I'm enjoying this trip."

"I was afraid you might be getting tired. I know you must be weary after your trip, and all."

"I'm not an old man yet, Quin. Are you only feeling the proper solicitude for your... Ahem... elder?" Tony returned, trying to hide the fact that he was really quite touched by the Quincy's sympathy, for he felt the feeling that lay under Quincy's words.

"Tony," Quincy began hesitantly, "can you tell me just what happened, and how?... Gee, I hope you don't mind," he added quickly.

"Of course not, Quin," Tony answered. "Please don't ask me to tell you the end, not just now. I promise that I will tell you all about it in detail before I leave."

"I know how you feel. It was a fool trick of mine to ask you. I was only curious. You know, I never saw her."

"I'll try to tell you what she was like. It's hard, though. I know you won't believe me when I say this, but she was the most wonderful girl in the world. You'll never have any idea how I miss her. It doesn't seem possible that I managed to live without her for all those years before we met each other.

"My life is so empty now. People say it's foolish for me to feel this way. I have all my life before me. Success, perhaps. Fame. But what good is all that without her? They would be empty honors without Marise to enjoy them too. No one can ever take her place. You know, no one can take your mother's place — so it is with me.

"I shall probably go on living in the same way, leading the same ordinary existence I would have had she lived. I'll probably meet many girls, some of them as beautiful as she, but they won't seem so beautiful to me. I will never find that dear companionship that I found in

Marise. I sometimes wonder why she was given to me at all, if she was to be taken away so soon. It was tantalizing, just that glimpse of what the future might have been. I know I sound like a blooming idiot, raving on this way. It's so hard.

"You have no idea what it means to me to be able to get all this off my chest. I had no one to talk with. Of course, the Teldons were there, but it was like trying to talk with one of those long-legged French dolls, to talk, I mean, really talk, to Kay Teldon. And Bob, oh, he's a good pal, but that's all he ever will be.

"Quin, if you knew how I wished you had been there. I don't know what I would have done if it hadn't been for that old German doctor, Doctor Frienheitz. He was like a father to me.

"Sometimes it seems to me that I just can't breathe because I want her so."

For a moment the air was vibrant with a deep current of sympathetic understanding. In the old, happy, pagan days, men were not ashamed to weep, but now we've become so civilized — and yet the savages practice stoicism, too.

Eleven o'clock. Big Ben in the tower was still lingering over the last mellow notes as Anthony and Quincy swung through the streets of one of the world's greatest capitals. Tony waved a familiar hand to Nelson standing on his column, black against the moon.

Soon they drew up in front of a tall, narrow house that loomed through the fog. The door opened, showing a red-orange rectangle of light with a man's figure silhouetted against it.

"Hi there, Pater," called Quincy. "I brought him."

"So glad to see you, my boy," he answered, coming down the steps. "Quincy has told me. If there is anything we can do — "

For a moment Tony's head swam. As if in a dream, he was transported back so that it seemed to him he was standing in front of another looming, black pile of masonry, shrouded in another fog, under another moon. He didn't see the figure of Jonathan Harker standing in a doorway illuminated by electric light. He was gazing with startled eyes on a tall figure who held a candle high in his hand... long, elastic shadows... a rich voice saying, "Welcome to my poor house..."

Then Anthony's head cleared. He collected himself and said,
"Thank you, Mr. Harker. Both you and Quincy have been so kind to me."

CHAPTER FIFTEEN

So for several days Anthony stayed with the Harkers. In the stress and occupation of his work, he, in a measure, forgot the many things that preyed on his mind in every waking hour. He realized how Time could dull pain and that forgetfulness would come with the years. Only when his eyes lit upon the little leather-covered volume that had been Marise's diary did the pang return to him. He loved that small book. It was the only intimate part of her that was left to him. Sometimes Tony would sit and read the notes Marise had made, and smile over her whimsical way of writing her impressions. But he carefully avoided reading her last entries. It would have been too heartbreaking to read the pages she had written during her delirium — as he firmly believed her illness to be.

One evening, the day before Tony was to start on his homeward journey, Mr. Harker, Quincy and he were sitting in front of the fire, talking.

"Well, Anthony," remarked Mr. Harker, "how will it seem, to be getting home again?"

"To tell the truth, sir, I am a trifle homesick. But I dread all the questions that will be asked. Some that I can't answer myself. You know how it will be: all my friends and relatives wanting to know all about this and that, all the morbid details. Really, I dread facing them," Tony answered.

"Yes, we knew how you would feel. That's why we tried not to seem too curious."

From the other side of the fireplace Quincy shot a somewhat shamefaced look at his father and grinned sheepishly at Tony. Tony smiled, too.

"Oh, no. I don't mind you. I feel you have a right to know. You invited me to come to your house and have treated me royally. How were you to know what made her die? Some contagious dreadful disease, she might have had. I do not know... I do not know."

And his voice trailed off as he watched the dancing flames, lost in retrospection.

"But, but... what was the matter?" Quincy asked impulsively.

"Son..." began his father.

"Just as I've said," answered Tony. "No one knows. At the beginning of the week she was perfectly well and happy, as far as we could see. She complained of nothing. She was in the best of spirits, the best of health. A week later, she was dead."

"But had she been doing anything that might have strained her heart? — providing, of course, that it was weak," asked Harker senior.

"No, we hadn't done anything of that sort. We climbed the mountain once. That is rather steep. I think perhaps the altitude might have affected her, as she did not sleep well towards the end."

"Very odd. Very odd, indeed."

"It was a terrible feeling to see her wasting away, day after day, knowing I could do nothing to save her. We had been living a very simple life there at the hotel, or rather the inn. We took your advice, you know, and stayed at "The Golden Krone". The only social life we had at that time was an occasional jaunt to one of the old castles thereabouts to visit a friend, or rather an acquaintance of ours, a Hungarian nobleman who lived in one of them. An interesting chap, if nothing else. I'll tell you about him sometime. Of course, the Teldons were there. You remember Kay Teldon, don't you, Quin?"

"Remember her? You bet I do!"

"She is quite unforgettable. As charming as she can be. Not as lovely as Marise was, though. But then, they were as different as night and day. That's a good mile. Risa was dark and gentle and tender, while Kay is gay and bright and dazzling.

"What I was going to say, though, was that you can imagine we had something to do anyway, with Kay around. It was her wild idea to explore those old castles at night. She got us into such a fix with one of them, though. We had broken in and were making ourselves quite at home when we discovered it was inhabited. We all felt awfully cheap. The owner was charming about it, a real good sport.

"A couple of days after that Marise began to fail."

"But," interposed Mr. Harker, "were there no symptoms that you could recognize? You should have called in a good doctor."

"That's just it, sir. We did. He was as mystified as we were. He could find nothing wrong. He sent to Buda-Pesth for another doctor. We had some of the best physicians in Germany at her bedside. And yet, as I have said, in a week, she died."

"But what did they call it? They must have had some name for her ailment?"

"No, nothing at all, except, the doctor remarked, when he first arrived, that she evidently suffered from pernicious anemia. This was followed by some sort of a breakdown, and I think Risa's sleepwalking might have had something to do with it."

"Her sleepwalking?"

"Yes. Towards the end she was bothered by bad dreams and at times she walked in her sleep. This was not a habit, as she said that she had never done such a thing before in her life, and it was quite unusual for her to have nightmares."

"Do you remember what the nightmares were about? Often some light is thrown on the working of the conscious mind by the fancies of the subconscious."

"Oh yes. She wrote them in her diary, which I kept, although she once tried to destroy it. They were horrible things, full of blood, and — oh, you should read it for yourself. I cannot make it clear. I sometimes wonder whether her dreams had any foundation in truth, or whether they were mere dreams. I know that you will think me crazy to believe them when you have seen her Diary."

"Bad dreams, did you say? Anemia, and loss of blood? If I dared think for one moment... but, no, it cannot be..."

"Yes, Mr. Harker. That is just the way she died. Loss of blood. Although there was no wound upon her body, and we all gave our blood for transfusions, she died."

Through the firelight Tony could see Mr. Harker's face, very white and drawn. Quincy rose and went over to his father's side and laid a hand on his shoulder. Mr. Harker asked, "Anthony Morrow, did anyone besides you, the doctors, and the Teldons know of your wife's illness?"

"Why, let me see. Oh yes, of course, our friend the Count had heard that she was ill."

"The Count?"

"You remember I spoke of this acquaintance. We spent some very pleasant evenings at his castle."

"What — what was his name?" Mr. Harker's voice was barely audible.

"Count Dracula."

In the silence that followed, Jonathan Harker slipped forward and fell from his chair in a faint. Quincy stood staring straight before him.

CHAPTER SIXTEEN

"Quick, Tony, hand me that bottle of brandy right there on the table. You'd better ring for Watkins... I don't know what..."

It was but a matter of minutes before Mr. Harker was laid on the leather-covered couch under the tender ministrations of Watkins, his valet, an ex-service man.

"Yes, sir, Mister Quincy," he agreed, "I think it's 'is 'eart. 'e's evidently 'ad a shock." Watkins looked accusingly from one young man to the other.

"I think I've heard that name before," Quincy reflected, his eyes glued on his father's ghastly face. Then, aloud, "Perhaps we'd better take him up to bed, you know. He'd be more comfortable there. If you'll give me a hand here, Tony, we can carry him."

They carried Mr. Harker slowly through the doorway, Watkins following with the decanter in his hand. After the patient had been carefully tucked in bed, Quincy telephoned for the doctor. The two young men talked in hushed voices as they waited for the physician to arrive. Anthony tried to figure out which part of their conversation would have given Mr. Harker such a start; Quincy tried to recall the name Tony had mentioned.

Ever since Quincy was a little lad he had heard the tale of his parents' youth, and had come to accept it as a family anecdote. He had never considered it as the truth, and his mother and father had not discussed it with him. To him, the characters involved were strange, mythical creatures, like his Uncle Irvin in the Indian Army, whom he had never seen. If one stopped to think, he must admit that they were human, and it had all probably transpired, but he had never taken sufficient interest to sit down and read the closely written sheets that had always lain in his father's desk drawer.

"Dracula.... Count Dracula.... where? — It's an odd thing, Tony. I feel a shiver run over me when I say that word. I feel as if at one time it meant something quite dreadful to me, rather like your "bogeyman," you know. If I remember it correctly, Dracula has something to do with an old family tale... The pater was in Hungary in eighteen ninety-something. Maybe Father knew him then."

"I don't believe so, Quin. This Count Dracula is not so old. He can't be more than 45 or 50 at the most. He'd have been pretty young when your father was there — why, just a mere baby. A man doesn't run in with a two-year old, you know. It might have been Dracula's father, though."

"It might, indeed. What was his name, did you say?"

"He had so many — let me see. He told us once, but one forgets. Ah, yes, I have it now. Arpad Voladya Greger, Van Betrich, Count Dracula — if that helps any."

"And I suppose he had a few extras to use in case of an emergency! What does a fellow want with so many names? I wonder what his wife says when she calls him to dinner?"

"There is no Countess Dracula."

"The doctor is 'ere, sir. Shall I show him up?" asked Watkins from the door.

"Oh yes. We won't mention this to the medico, if you don't mind, Tony. There's no need to drag family matters into this."

After a brief examination the doctor pronounced the patient out of danger, explaining that it was merely a case of shock, and that Mr. Harker would soon recover. Before the doctor left, Mr. Harker regained consciousness. He followed Anthony across the room with fear-stricken eyes and motioned the doctor out of the room.

"Don't try to talk, Pater, just rest."

"Son...my desk....upper drawer...key...pocket."

With a knowing look at Tony, Quincy hurried from the room.

ANTHONY'S DIARY

After Quincy came back with the manuscript his father had sent for, he told me to take it, read it, and to give my candid opinion as to whether or not I believed it to be true.

"May I read it, too, Father?" asked Quincy. "I have never seen it at all, you know."

"Yes," said the man on the bed. "It is only right that you should hear the story I know to be true. Now, when I read the account of that terrible year, it does not seem possible that such things could ever be. All those mentioned in the book are dead. All except myself. Would that I had died as they did. Peacefully. Content. As it is, in my old age, I learn I must go down to my grave knowing the work to which I gave my youth was all in vain, that I was powerless to save the one I loved and, worst of all, that there still lives on earth the most malignant enemy mankind ever had.

"I charge you, my son. This will be your duty: Read that book. And with the last drop of your blood, fight to wipe Dracula from this world.

"Mina, Mina. How could I have known? We thought we had conquered... Mina."

I will never forget that scene as long as I live. Mr. Harker seemed to have aged years in just these few minutes. He has always had white hair, or at least as long as I can remember. He had an accident in his youth, I believe. He was so terribly earnest, and kept calling his wife's name. It was quite a time before Quincy and I could quiet him, but when he was at last still, he seemed to sink into the farthest depths of morbid despair.

Personally, I believe that he had a stroke, apoplexy. He must be getting along in years and it's not improbable that this was the cause of his fit of insensibility. I still can see the look of terror that came over his face, that absolute helplessness, that despair when I said the name. I realize now it must have been the Count that he feared and dreaded so. That was why he was so startled.

After Mr. Harker was settled for the night, Quincy and I went downstairs to read the manuscript. We poked the fire 'til it blazed up again, laid in quite a supply of tobacco and made ourselves as comfortable as possible. I could see we were in for a night of reading. That's a pleasant way to while away the long dark hours when you are lonely if no other companion is near.

The packet of papers seemed to be made up of letters, notes, and extracts from diaries, all carefully typed by Mrs. Harker. They seemed to be quite old, as some of the papers were yellowed with age. Nothing, however, seems aged to me now, after the castle. That was a real treasure trove of antiques.

Ho hum! Well, here goes... Mr. Harker's trip to Transylvania... So, that's where the Count comes in...

ANTHONY'S DIARY Continued
Later

Here it is early morning and the light of day never shone on a man as puzzled and afraid as I. If for one moment I dared to believe that which is written here in Mr. Harker's papers, I believe that I should go mad. To think that this might be true!

Poor Quincy is as upset as I. His own parents went through what I am facing now and swear that everything inscribed in those pages actually happened.

But a million questions are teeming in my brain. Is this Count Dracula in the Harkers' notes the same man Risa and I knew? How can it be? Mr. Harker says himself that he killed the Count with his own hands. If that's true, how can he live on, carrying on his dreadful work? It is not true. It cannot be. God would not allow such a creature to live. Yet how can so many people be mistaken? Is there not some bit of truth at the bottom of all these ancient superstitions? The superstitions of today are the facts of yesterday. Why is it that there are some who are fabled to have had more than mortal strength, to have lived for centuries and not died and passed away as have all other men? These and a million more questions are beating in my brain, but must all go unanswered. I cannot trust myself to think of them.

Suppose that Risa was... and her own diary, that so closely parallels all that is in this manuscript. These were dreams, they could not be anything else. The men and women who wrote these papers were mad, or else I am.

One thought overwhelms me. If Risa was — undead — if I found her, would I have the courage to mutilate her, to kill her, to stop the evil? I cannot believe it. For all our sakes, and most of all for the value of my own sanity, I dare not credit this preposterous story. How dreadfully concrete, so undeniable is the written word both in her journal and my own, and here, to cap the climax, this manuscript! I must deny the possible, improbable totally preposterous, and yet...

CHAPTER SEVENTEEN

Late that afternoon, Mr. Harker called Quincy and Anthony into his bedroom. He had them sit in two large chairs, drawn up close to him, so the three could converse easily.

"Well, Anthony, what do you think of this story? Do you believe it could be true?"

"No, sir, I do not believe it. Or at least I dare not admit even to myself that such a thing might be."

"Do you, Quincy?"

"Well, Pater, that is rather hard on me, don't you think? I can't very well doubt your word, can I? I've been brought up with that, well, drilled into me, as it were. I think in some ways it's a pretty stiff story for a modern, sensible, well-educated person to credit. I'll admit that one can't explain some of the things that happened without accepting it. Just the same, I think you and this Doctor chap went into it rather deep. It's really just too beastly."

"Too beastly. Well, son, perhaps you are right. But how would you feel if you knew such a man existed? Or if you saw your mother dying by inches, fading away, day after day?..."

"Don't!" begged Tony.

"Yes, you know how it is. So it was with me. But I was not afraid to believe. I tried to face the facts and to conquer them if I could. I thought I had succeeded, but I find I did not."

"Yes, Mr. Harker. That's what's been puzzling me. If you had killed Count Dracula, as you said you did, how is it that he is alive (I guess one would use that term) today?"

"Yes, Pater, how do you account for that?"

"As I have said, some things are beyond all human explanations. That is the story, or rather the account of our adventures. And if you are half the man I think you are, Anthony Morrow, you will set out to avenge your wife's murder. For he killed her as surely as if he had fired a gun at her, or given her poison. It is not only her corporeal death — we must all face that sooner or later — but it is her spiritual end. Do you realize —" the elderly man raised himself from his pillow with a dangerous light of fanaticism burning in his sunken eyes.

"You really must be quiet, Father, you know. I think if we leave you, perhaps you could get some sleep," interrupted Quincy, much to Tony's relief.

"Sleep? Sleep, did you say? There are things more important than sleep to be considered just now, young man. I never expect to get out of this bed. I know my end is drawing near, and that it is quite" — this with a wan smile — "unavoidable. I'm not afraid. But before I go I want to see Anthony started on the only road that can bring him consolation and peace. Think what it will mean to him to go through life tortured with doubt and always wondering if this could be true?"

"Please, Pater..."

"Silence. I want you and Anthony to go back to Transylvania, to wipe out this monster.

I want you to finish the work I started so many years ago. It will be dangerous and perhaps it will be a waiting game. But I know you can do it.

"Will you promise a dying man to carry out a work done for your own good? Will you, Anthony Morrow?"

"But Mr. Harker, how can you ask it? I couldn't bear to go back to that land, with this mission in mind, such a solemn purpose. I believe I'd go mad! Would you go there, Quin?"

"I? Why should I go? To tell the truth — although I confess I do believe this Dracula business might be more than wild theory — I see no reason why I should go, unless, of course, you want me to go, Tony."

"Do you realize what you're saying, my son? Stop to consider what fate might be your Mother's at this very moment!"

"But I can't get into it that far, Father. I really am not capable of setting aside all my beliefs about life and death on such a short notice."

"I want you to go. This is all I ask. If you can see the Count in the daytime, see him eat or drink or be reflected in a looking glass, or even throw a shadow, I am content. You can come home. But try to wrestle with him. If he cannot throw you both with the greatest ease, come home, I say. I will believe that all this never happened. The only reason you didn't know all the story as you grew up was that we wanted to wait until you were older so you would have a clear, mature view of the affair.

"I now am putting it up to you. Test it for yourselves. Will you do that?"

Finally Tony turned from the window, looked at the man on the bed and said, "I will."

"I'm with you, as you'd say, Tony," replied his friend.

"God bless you both," returned his father from the shadow of the canopy.

ANTHONY'S DIARY

I spent the day packing my trunk again. It seems I'm doomed to spend my days traveling from one place to another.

I really dread going back to Transylvania — not so much the physical danger as the memories that it holds for me. The thought of staying in "The Golden Krone," perhaps in the very same room that we had before, is all too much! To think I'll once again spend sleepless nights watching the bats wheel around the moon, as Risa and I used to, or to spend my days beside her grave — Oh, I must tell Mr. Harker I cannot go through with this.

Later

No, I can't back out of it now. I must carry this mission to its end, whatever that might be.

We have decided that Quincy will go under another name, masquerading as an American. He says he's been around me long enough to be able to carry it off without making a fool of himself. He is now trying to accustom himself to the new name of Stanley Morton. All his luggage has to be remarked so that there will be no "Q.A.H"'s to embarrass us on our journey.

All the million and one details of the trip have been taken off our hands by Mr. Harker's secretary. That is a great relief, especially when it is a trip such as this one, for which I have no taste.

Transylvania. If anyone had told me three days ago that I would so soon be going back, I would have called him crazy. I think we're all a little crazy!

CHAPTER EIGHTEEN

We took the plane at the airport and started across the Channel. It was quite calm and there was nothing of note to record on the passage. It was the oddest feeling to watch ships nonchalantly swimming directly beneath us. This was the first time I've crossed the Channel by air, but after this, any vessel is too slow for me. I pray I may never be compelled to come back to Europe again. Of all the parts of the world, this is the one that hurts me most to return to.

Quincy has entire charge of this trip. I am merely a silent partner. He has arranged for our transportation and has even reserved our quarters at different hotels.

He has insisted that we stop for a few days in Paris. He believes from his father's notes that it would be best if we wait for awhile and prepare ourselves both spiritually and materially for the coming battle. It doesn't seem possible to me that this can be anything but a terrible nightmare. Quincy has taken care that we are armed with pistols as well as crosses.

I have gathered from Mr. Harker's notes and the notes of those brave men who have spent part of their lives trying to kill Dracula that it would not be possible for Dracula to take Risa unless it were her will. Madame Mina speaks of that, I remember. It is brought up in the notes so many times. That is all very well. But Risa would not leave me. If any of this is true, that is the hinge on which it turns. She was my wife, my very own. And I know that she loved me with all her heart and soul. She cannot be that which Quincy believes.

ANTHONY MORROW'S DIARY Continued

Another dreary day. We set out from Paris in a dismal fog. My whole life seems to be wrapped in the mists of doubt and ignorance. If we only knew what to believe... and what is mere folly to entertain for even a moment.

The whole world is made up of everlasting railroad tracks, retreating monotonously into the distance. The throbbing rhythm of the train pounds maddeningly in my ears. To Quin, this work is exhilarating but to me it is all quite terrifying. It admits the existence of such a being, and to me it is all impossible.

Quincy theorizes that if we were to visit the vault where I buried Risa, we could tell if there was any necessity to carry on with our work of destruction. I, however, am opposed to having the vault opened. I am not so advanced along the path of credulity as to consent to such a thing.

Poor Quin, he often complains that I am but a lukewarm helper and not really in this work with all my heart and soul. If this Dracula thing is true, I shall be inclined to doubt the very existence of a deity or a future life.

Every inch that I advance towards Transylvania seems like squeezing out drops of blood.

Looking at this whole thing calmly, as a twentieth century, sane man would, I find it impossible to believe that a man like the Count could be the terrible monster that Mr. Harker would have me think.

The miles and hours passed swiftly, even for Tony, and one evening they arrived in Buda-Pesth. Here again they stopped for a final checkup on all their supplies, or as Quincy called them, their "armaments."

Much to Tony's disgust, Quincy insisted that they stay in Buda-Pesth for several days so that, at least for Quincy, they might get some pleasure out of the trip.

"You know, Tony, there is no reason why we should make ourselves miserable over the whole thing. This is the second time I've been here, but only the first time I can remember. You've had a chance to really become acquainted with the people and customs here, but I haven't. Try to forget the morbid side of all this for awhile and let me enjoy myself. I haven't overlooked the fact that we've come here with a serious purpose in mind. But surely there can be no harm in going someplace tonight and having a change of atmosphere."

It was as hard to deny Quincy Harker something as it would have been to make him do something he didn't want to do, so that night Tony and Quincy went to the heart of the city in search of entertainment. In one of the largest and most luxurious cabarets that Buda-Pesth could boast, they sat down to watch the crowd. Quincy was in high spirits that evening and regaled his somewhat somber companion with sprightly comments about the passersby.

"There," he remarked, "notice the gentleman on your left. Why, Tony, I said your left, not right. Can't you tell his whole history? You see? He is a farmer. He has made quite a bit of money and he came here to spend it. That is his wife beside him. How do I know she's his wife? Tony! Can't you see the fellow would like to smile at that lovely blonde but he's afraid the wife will see him? And the blonde's a beauty, Tony. I'll smile at her myself.

"And there, my friend. That's an old maid who's come here for her health. Notice the poodle with the embroidered jacket. She will feed it a bit of that chicken in a moment, after carefully seeing there are no bones on which her little precious might choke! Why is it that those dogs never choke?

"But Tony, she isn't here," he remarked with a sigh.

"Who isn't here?" asked Tony disinterestedly.

"Why, my ideal, of course. The ideal girl of this country. Blonde, perhaps, or else as dark as a gypsy. A stunning creature. Considering that same blonde, she might do in a pinch, but I could do better with time.

"Why did you come here on your honeymoon, Tony? You should have come before. Oh, yes. Much before... Forgive me. I didn't think. I really am so very sorry."

The meal continued in silence, unbroken until Quincy ventured, "Not really angry, are you, Tony?"

"No," he answered slowly.

"I understand I really put my foot into it, old man. You know how I feel. I-I would give anything to take those words back."

"Oh, that's all right, Quin. The last time I was here I was with Risa, and to be here again without her is almost more than I can bear. I suppose it's a good thing... I was afraid of how I'd feel when we got to "The Golden Krone." This way it will not be so hard. In a way, I'm getting used to living without her."

"It's lonely, I know, Tony. But we must hold on to the hope that...."

"You mean that she may still be alive? Don't be silly, Quin. Besides, if there is any truth in these mad stories, what good would it do me if she were not dead? What is it you call it? Undead?"

"You still don't believe, do you, Tony? I can't say I blame you. Under the circumstances, I'd be pretty skeptical myself. If my —" and he broke off suddenly with a smile of complete satisfaction on his face.

"What is it, Quin? Have you suddenly discovered the secret of the universe?"

"No. But I have discovered something that is quite wonderful just now. There behind you is my ideal Hungarian."

Tony shrugged.

"What! You crazy beast. You won't even turn around?"

"No, Quin. I'm not interested. There's only one girl for me. It doesn't make any difference whether she's Hungarian, or, say, an English girl."

"But Tony... Oh well. But you can't stop me from describing her. I wonder what her escort is like. He probably doesn't deserve her at all. I can't see him. Why do they plant trees in these places so you can't see across the way? That's funny. There's a mirror over there, too. He must be under the table?"

"Look out, old chap. You're liable to get a stiff neck."

"Yes. And he probably isn't worth it, either. I must say she's the loveliest thing I've laid eyes on for a long, long time. Did I say a blonde? Oh, no... I always have said that my ideal was a brunette. I do like a dark girl in black, at least one with a complexion like that. Oh, Tony, don't be an ass. Do turn around."

"Why? I don't care if she is one of these cozy brunettes with a 'peaches-and-cream' complexion."

"That's a fine description, of somebody else. She's not at all what one would call cozy. If she is one of those comforts around the house, well, so is an iceberg. She's tall and dark and as pale as ivory. As a rule I don't care for those exotic makeups but she is striking, with her pale face and blood-red lips. She doesn't seem to be a very pleasant sort, though. (Turn around, you idiot.) She sends the shivers up and down my spine. Just the same....she's beautiful!"

"Oh, do stop raving and pay some attention to your dinner."

"And her hair, Tony. It is so blue-black — just like one of those grapes when they're wet after a rain — so shiny."

"Quin, please. For your own sake, I ask you to stop staring. Do you realize that you're making a spectacle of yourself?"

"But Tony — "

"Oh, come on!"

And so poor Quincy was unwillingly dragged off to the hotel and made to pack for the coming trip into the mountains. "I shall not soon forgive you, Tony. I only leave here under protest. And you would, too, if you hadn't acted like an idiot and refused to turn around. I don't care, though. She didn't like you, either. She looked up and saw you, spoke to the man she was with, and got ready to leave."

ANTHONY'S DIARY
The next morning

Off to the mountains. The same old trip. Poor Quincy did hate to leave here. But if we're to go through with all this hocus-pocus business of trying to drive away a devil, I hope to get it over with as soon as possible. When this is finished, I will be free to go home and try to lose myself in my work. I have so many plans for the future that must be changed. There is still a faint feeling of unreality that pervades all that I attempt to do.

There, it's time to start. May I have the strength to go through with this. And please, dear God, may the end come quickly.

CHAPTER NINETEEN

ANTHONY'S DIARY

Off to Bitzritz. I dread the last few miles! I feel, however, that it won't be as hard as I expect. I am afraid at times that I am an awful coward about this whole business. Poor Quin is beginning to feel rather nervous himself. It may be that we are going into danger, but I guess we can face it.

Later

We took the diligence from B. I am writing this as we go. The windows of "The Golden Krone" are now barely visible through the fog. Oh, the endless fog, fog, fog! I think I could like this country even now, except for this everlasting mist. In the distance I again hear the howling of the wolves.

It seems to me that I can almost feel her presence. As we passed the little graveyard at Bitzritz, I felt an overwhelming wave of loneliness, and now as we are entering the country road of the inn I almost believe that she is here beside me once more.

Here comes the innkeeper!

Inside the inn, the travelers warmed themselves before a roaring fire, as the innkeeper hurried to prepare their rooms.

"The gentleman will have the same room?" he asked.

Tony nodded in assent. What else was there to do? Indeed, he controlled his feelings well until he again found himself in the room where Risa had died. Then, for the first time since he had left London, he gave his thoughts full reign. With a poignant pain, he remembered all that had happened in that room. Yes, he thought, as he stepped out on to the balcony where he had found her that fatal night, it is still the same. He even thought he could see her smiling at him from the mist that smoked and writhed in the beam of light that glowed outward from the lamp. Still the same... the same moon struggling through the fog, still those huge bats that were attracted by the light and wheeled and circled just beyond his reach.

"Well, Tony. It's too thick to see much of the castle tonight," Quincy said.

"Yes," Tony agreed absently. "Too dark."

"In the morning the sun will probably take care of that. No doubt it'll be as clear as can be tomorrow."

"It takes the morning sun to clear away the fog. But Quin, why is it that the morning is so long in coming?"

"It isn't so far away at that," returned Quincy, glancing at his watch.

"In the daylight I think I can see my way clear of this hopeless muddle of uncertainty. Tonight it's so dark, so dark."

"Go to sleep, old man. You'll feel so much better for a good night's rest."

"Probably. Good night, Quin."

"Good night, Tony."

Anton, the innkeeper's little grandson, was sitting on the steps of the inn. In the dust before him he had been tracing pictures with a stick.

"Here," he fancied to himself, "is the castle. And this is the roadway. Down the road comes a coach, with two, no, four great, big, milk-white horses. In the coach is a lovely princess with long, dark hair. I wish..." and he broke off, absorbed in his own thoughts.

"Someday, someday she will come — or maybe a fairy princess on a big black charger. And she will say to me: 'Don't you want to visit me in the castle? I have many things that little boys like to play with and there are so many good things in my kitchen!'

"And then I will climb into her coach, and we will roll off to the castle on the hill... just like that one, but it will be much grander, with servants and all the carpets of velvet, and we will eat off a golden platter studded with jewels, and it will sparkle like father's watch when we go to church on Sundays."

For a moment he was distracted from his dream as a brisk breeze wiped out his little sketch, but the sight of the distant ruin on the hill, standing black against the sunset, recalled him.

"Yes," he decided, "I shall go. And then when I am a man I shall be king and have a royal palace of my own. And it will be twice as grand as any that have been built here on earth before!"

"I wonder, though, if I will know her, the fairy princess? But of course. When she comes clattering in to the courtyard and calls to me, I shall say, 'Good day, Your Highness. I have been expecting you. Will you wait until I say good-bye?'"

The thought of leaving his parents, though, disturbed him, and the tears welled up in his eyes as he sat, half hidden in the deepening dusk. As he was manfully stifling a sob, he heard a voice call from the darkness behind him, "What is the matter, little lad?"

With a start, he turned to find... yes, it must be she... his fairy princess!

"Do you suppose we could possibly take Mother and Father with us?" he asked, vaguely disappointed that she should have arrived without the horses and the golden coach.

"With us, where, dear?"

"To the castle, of course."

"Would you like to see the castle where I live?"

"Oh, yes! But that is why you came, isn't it? You knew that I was expecting you, didn't you? Where are the horses?" and he stood up, childishly forgetting even his parents in the companionship of this most delightful lady, who seemed to anticipate his very wishes.

"The horses... oh. They are in their stable up at the castle. If you come with me, you shall see them."

"Must we walk? Is it far? Am I coming home again, soon?"

"Oh, yes. As soon as you wish."

"Then I won't say good-bye to my family. And when I come back, you must come and see me."

"In the inn?"

"Yes. Shall I come now?"

"Yes... we must start."

Out on the water a vessel moved cautiously through the mists sounding her inquiring siren hoarsely.

Fog! Fog! The entire world seemed to consist of dun, swirling shapes that hovered over the ship and strove with futile, strengthless fingers to impede her blind progress.

Twilight settled over the countryside like a gray pall. None of the usual golden-red lights gleamed a cheery "good night," but a few wan wisps filtered through the clouds like pale nuns bidding the earth a last resigned farewell.

Through the ruined walls of the castle on the hill the fog wove and gained entrance through the shattered clerestory windows, writhing across the smoke-blackened beams. Its stale, musty scent even pervaded the chapel and mingled with the unutterable stench of ruin and decay.

Silence hung heavy in the chapel, silence as thick within as the mist without. Even the furry spiders hung motionless in their dust-covered webs as if in fear of breaking it. Bats hung clustered in the corners, still as the moldering bones in those ponderous coffins. And yet — there was a sound, though not one of the pale slimy beetles had scuttled across the moldering wall. Again, a creaking, and a coffin lid moved. A long prehensile hand groped along its edge and then a figure arose from within the coffin. It was Dracula.

Instantly, Life — if one could call it that — invaded that hall of Death. The spiders retreated to their corners. Disturbed, dormant bats whirred upward, beating their membraned wings against the roof.

Silently, Dracula stepped to the other coffin on the dais and opened the lid to find Marise smiling up at him. Her arms rose to him as he lifted her out, and so they stood for a moment, cold cheek to cheek. Ghastly salutation, embrace of corpses, yet living cadavers. Every human impulse gone, yet there existed for them a strange union in this living death.

They moved out into the upper hall of the castle. There in the octagonal room, amid the candles and fire glow, one could but note again Marise's beauty. More than ever, her skin and teeth gave the impression of fragile translucence, augmented by the feverish brilliance of her eyes and the darkness of her hair. She threw herself down on the wolf-skin-covered couch and turned restlessly from side to side.

"Are you going abroad tonight?"

"Yes," he answered. "You are coming with me."

"I am tired... yet restless. What is the matter with me? What is it I want?"

"Tonight you shall see. Yes, in a few hours the time should be right."

Two dim shapes flowed out into the night, scarcely more concrete than the fog that veiled them. Two bats wheeled and floated above the little knot of houses that lay below.

In one, a soft light glowed in an upper window. A young child lay asleep, lulled and comforted by the small shaded lamp that stood at his bedside. The bats dipped lower. The curtain of the window moved with a rustle and Marise and Dracula stood within.

"He's... asleep?" she whispered.

"Yes. You will not awaken him."

The woman moved forward and bent over the child. He was lying with his head thrown back, his arms folded on the covers. Her face was nearly on the pillow now, her eyes on the pulse that beat in the side of his throat. It fascinated her, that movement... up, down... one, two... It must stop. It had to! Her eyes became fixed, her nostrils dilated, her throat contracted, and then, with a gasp, she threw herself forward. Her mouth touched his neck — how soft the flesh was. There it was, still beating, beating, under her lips. She pressed harder, but still that measured throbbing. She was pressing so hard now that her teeth hurt against her lips. She drew her lips apart and then that soft skin was between her teeth. How odd human flesh tasted! Harder, harder — there! Her teeth were through and the blood welled up against her tongue, salty, sharp. How familiar — yes, the night — the Mystic Sacrament!

Thirstily she drank until a hand on her shoulder roused her.

"Come. It is enough."

Unwillingly she turned away and wiped her mouth.

At the window she turned and looked back at the lad on the bed. She laughed.

"It was good, good. And now, I am content."

From the castle window she watched the dawn hesitantly venture across the hills, and she lay down with a tired sigh.

The next night she went, and again. Never again did Dracula go with her.

One night, nearly a week later, she turned from her repast as dawn neared, and knocked the lamp from the table on which it stood. She heard hurrying footsteps in the corridor and she hurled herself at the window as the door flew open.

She could hear a man's howl of rage and grief. His words were flung at her through the night.

"I know you. I know you for the foul thing you are! My son, my son, I shall save you."

An anxious father hurried desperately up the hill to the castle. It was the only possible conclusion. His son had been seen, yes. The child had gone towards the castle ruin in the company of a woman. Now who could she be? What human being would dare to enter that place after nightfall?

"There are many in this world that are not human," he thought gloomily.

Then all of a sudden he realized that he had passed through the narrow doorway in the walls of the hills that made the castle such an excellent place of fortification. With a last deep breath to summon his courage, he threw himself against the door that was slightly open. It gave under his hands and he found himself in the great hall.

The hall was faintly illuminated by the moonlight that had filtered through the cracks and crannies in the wall and made the flagstone floor a mosaic of silver and onyx.

There, a darker spot on the stones, lay his son, asleep and very quiet. It was but a moment until he had gathered the child into his arms and fled towards the door, but he was stopped on the very threshold. A woman was blocking the doorway, her eyes blazing with anger.

"Drop him!" she ordered. "He shall stay here until I am through with him."

With a cry the father sprang forward, but as he sought to grasp her, she was gone, reappearing a few feet away. As he tried for the second time to lay his hands upon her she called softly, and in an instant a tall figure appeared beside her.

In his anguish Anton's father did not hear it, but down in the village there was a gentle chime of bells. At the climax of the Benediction service, Father Adelbert, the old priest, stepped to the door of the church, holding the jeweled monstrance that contained the Holy Wafer. The blessings went out from the church.

At this moment, Anton's father felt himself dealt a mighty blow. Then suddenly, he found himself outside the door, dazed, bruised, but safe, with the child beside him.

"Let him go. We are strong, but there are times when we are weak."

ANTHONY'S DIARY
The next morning

I slept very well last night, except for the fact that someone was ill in the inn. I could hear people moving about until almost morning. I understand that the innkeeper's little grandson is not well.

In this bright light the castle can be seen distinctly from the windows of the inn. It appears to be unchanged, presenting that same desolate look that it had several months ago. Quincy and I are going to reconnoiter this afternoon. I hope we'll be able to see the Count today and end this waiting.

The countryside stretches upward toward the mountains with the same air of peace and happiness. It doesn't seem possible that so many dreadful things could happen in this lovely spot.

In the late afternoon two figures could be seen toiling up the slopes of the road that led up to the castle. As they reached the top, there was a moment of indecision before they attacked the huge door.

"If he is here, I rather think it would be the thing to knock, don't you?"

"Of course, Quin. We can try the housebreaking stunt if there is no answer. You might try around in the back. Here, take this lamp. You may need it as it is as black as night back there. If I remember correctly, the stables are down there to the right. Yes, that's the way."

Quincy vanished down one of the dark archways with a flashlight in one hand and a revolver in the other. Soon he returned to report that all was quiet and he had been unable to rouse anyone.

"There were no servants at the castle," Tony remembered. "No. Wait a moment. There was a coachman. I noticed that he was the only one around here except the Count himself."

"Well, he isn't here now. I went in as far as I could. I found the two horses. Beautiful animals. There was no sign of a man. There was food and water left out for them but there was no groom."

"I'm afraid that we'll have to break in, then. All set, Quin? These doors are pretty hard to move."

A creak, a groan — the huge portals swung open to reveal what the future held in store for them.

Slowly they entered the great hall and without stopping, moved toward the huge staircase. Cautiously they made their way to the top.

"Now, which way?" asked Quincy in a hushed voice.

"Here. This is the room. Over there is the one that Risa loved so much. I will rap here. I wonder?...."

"No answer. It's evident the place is deserted. Shall we explore a bit?"

"Let me see those notes. If this is all true, Dracula will probably be in his coffin in the chapel. It is downstairs somewhere, I gather."

Silently they descended the stairs and faced the three dark archways at their foot.

"Eenie, meenie, miney, mo... Take your choice." Quincy was trying to hide his real anxiety.

"We ought to have brought stronger lights. The battery in mine has gone dead already. A man could very easily get lost in those tunnels. We can't tell where they lead or which is the one we're looking for. In this crumbling old ruin, it probably wouldn't be safe to walk in there. Our footsteps might cause it to cave in."

"My father went in there."

"Yes, but Quin, he knew where he was going. We don't. That was fifty years ago, almost. In that time, who knows what has happened in this building. Fifty years of storms and wind, possibly an earthquake... as I say, this is not safe.

"Quin, give up the mad idea. It cannot, cannot be true. You will admit yourself that it is utterly fantastic!"

"There's some truth in that. The idea that the walls of the place are not safe wouldn't stop me, I'd go on exploring — but look, it's getting late. We wasted so much time knocking, and snooping around there in back took quite a while. It will be sunset any moment now. I, for one, am not going to stay in this bat-infested ruin after dark with one defective flashlight. Come on!"

In the eerie silence that precedes the end of day, Tony and Quincy returned to the inn.

As they stepped inside, Quincy remarked," I am going back there tomorrow. Will you come?"

"Why? In the name of Common Sense, can you give me one good reason? Will you say, 'You must return to that impossible ruin and see if your wife is there, lying an undead ghoul? You must return and kill the man that lives there, because of an old fairy tale?' Would you expect any sane man to believe all you've said? Do you think you can convince me that my wife is a demon, a horrid thing that lives after death by preying on the blood of others, that she is a thing accursed, polluted, unclean?"

"Tony, Tony, can't you see what I mean? You promised my father...."

"I promised your father that I would come back to this terrible land. I said I would do that much, and I have done it. But I cannot agree with your credulous view about the super-natural. I am not willing to let this thing go any farther."

"Tony, if you would only go to her tomb, we could soon tell. I am only asking you to do this to prove it to yourself."

"And if she is in her tomb, what then?"

"If she is truly dead, we will return to England. If she is not..."

"Well, if she is not?"

"I shall kill her."

"How?"

"By driving a stake through her body, cutting off the head and stuffing the mouth with garlic or wolf bane."

"Quincy Harker, you are mad. You must be crazy to suggest this thing to me. I will not even permit the sacrilege of opening the tomb. If you had suggested something sensible, I would consent. But to think of mutilating her dear body that way, in that way!"

"Won't you even consent to my looking in the tomb?"

"No."

"Tony, I am only trying to save you all the pain I can. You know this question will torment you all your life. This alone can cause your agony to cease. Tony, please!"

"No."

"Gentlemen!" It was the innkeeper who had just entered.

"May I be so bold, my little grandson, he is very ill and he is sleeping. The noise..."

"Of course. I remember now." Tony was his usual self again. "I am so sorry. Is there anything we can do? We would only be too glad to be of any assistance. What is the matter with the little chap?"

Immediately all expression was wiped from the face of the innkeeper. He crossed himself as he said in a low voice.

"I do not know."

CHAPTER TWENTY

ANTHONY MORROW'S DIARY

Poor lad. I begged the innkeeper to let me see him and he took us up to the little room at the back. The child was lying in bed, so pale and wan that he reminded me of Risa. It is evidently the same disease. He must be about five years old, quite a handsome little fellow, with dark hair and large dark eyes.

He was sleeping heavily as we entered and merely opened his eyes when his mother spoke to him.

She explained that he, too, was restless at night, afraid to be left alone, and always very weak in the morning. They had tried to cure him with all the cures they knew but it seemed quite hopeless. I offered to send for a doctor from the city but they declined. I then suggested that I might be able to do something, but they again refused. As his grandfather said,

"The doctor, what good is he? And you? You could not even save the one most dear to you."

I would do anything to save the child. He is so like my Risa, and as he sleeps he even has her expression. Another reason: if I can save one life that is afflicted with this dreadful disease, in a way it will redeem Risa's life. I know what Quincy thinks.

"You cannot save that baby with medicines," was all he said when he saw the boy.

Quincy believes if I need any further proof of Dracula's evil ways, this is it. I laughed at him. It is not true. I am as certain of that as he is that it is all as his father wrote it. At first I was inclined to believe and Quincy was the doubter; now, our opinions are reversed.

The only service I can do these people is to sit up with the child tonight. They are all tired out from weeks of watching over him; I can relieve them of that worry, at least.

Later

I am settled here for the night, with my pipe and book. I can regale a few minutes by writing in my diary. Before she left, Anton's mother thanked me with tears in her eyes.

"You, too, sir, know the sadness of watching over one who has been kissed by the awful vampyr. You know we cannot fight them with mortal strength. Had we only known that your lady..." she broke off and turned away.

"It is too late for me," I replied. "I only hope I may help save my little namesake, here."

She came to me and made the sign of the cross on my forehead. "His mother blesses you. Here." She reached into her pocket and took out a little cross made of a strand of palm. "From Palm Sunday," she said. "May the blessed cross of Palm preserve you from harm."

I thanked her and slipped it here, into the pages of my diary.

In the silence here all is peaceful. The only sound is Anton's breathing and the flutter of bats' wings outside. It is clear tonight and the moonlight is strong.

The bats are wheeling so near this evening. It must be monotonous being a bat. All there is to do is to hang by one's heels all day and chase your shadow around the moon all night. Ugh, that big fellow was close. I believe if I had stretched out my hand I could have touched him. Their eyes are phosphorescent, like a cat's. I wonder if those larger ones are some different species? They seem to be different from the rest. They are certainly bolder.

Ho, hum! There is that fog again. A thin ribbon of mist is drifting across the window... I ought to have had a nap! I think I will lie down awhile, but it's stuffy in here. I'll open a window first...

Silence... only the deep breathing of the watcher and the watched. In through the open window the fog stole in silver wisps, thicker and thicker. The wreath of flowers that had been around the boy's neck was lying on the floor where Tony had placed them when the lad complained of his throat hurting him.

The room was blue now, with the mist. A candle which burned dimly at the other end of the room could barely be seen, the flame surrounded with a rainbow, as the light glowed through the moisture.

Then the fog seemed to be gone, the candle went out, and only the moonlight lying in pale splotches on the floor illuminated the room. A dark, cloaked figure hovered over the bed, a soft sigh and a smothered cry...

Deep down in his inner consciousness Anthony remembered that there was some reason why he must stay awake. Some duty... but sleep was so enticing. He needed rest. But something forbade him to lie there in the dark. A duty, a trust. What was it? If only he could open his eyes he would remember, but they were so heavy, heavy. And it was pleasant to lie there in the quiet. Finally a soft cry awoke him, just enough so that he had to open his eyes. There... he remembered... it all came back... The boy... the boy was calling to him...

With a start he was upright... but even as consciousness returned, he realized that there was someone else in the room. He sensed the presence immediately. Without calling out he quietly reached for the candle. Oh, where was it? Every instinct seemed to whisper, "Hurry, hurry." Each silence cautioned, "Softly, softly." There. He had the candle and his lighter. He prayed a little wordless prayer in the darkness, that the lighter would work, silently and at once. Oh, blessed light!

The figure beside the bed turned and, as he looked, Anthony Morrow felt the darkness close once more about him. As with a swift rush of cold air, it was gone, leaving his tortured cry of "Risa!" ringing in the empty room.

CHAPTER TWENTY-ONE

There he stood — tall, still, one arm on the mantelpiece, the flames throwing weird shadows across his pallid face.

With a cry, Anthony leaped forward, but with one sweep of his arm, Dracula threw him to the floor.

"Oh, you fools! You blind and puny fools! Did you think that you could conquer me? I, who led Armies before your father's father was born? Hah! Have I not shown that I was all-powerful? Even those you love are mine. Your wife, whom you adored — she is my Countess — and you, you are her cast-off lover. For centuries, my curse will be upon you.

"You over there, with your pale face so like your mother's, she whom once I wanted. So you, too, would try to cheat me! Because you took those two women in another lifetime — Lucy and Mina — you start. Eh, I thought so, because of your father. For half a century I laid dead, but when I awoke, I found the one for whom I have waited all these centuries. Because Jonathan Harker saved his wife and her friend, I had to lie in my coffin, true dead for fifty long years. But I have returned.

"Now you," and he touched Anthony with his foot, "because you have saved that boy, Marise whom you loved must be true dead for awhile, and I, too, because she is of my making."

"How did you escape my father?" Quincy demanded.

"That man who tried to kill me shall die in torture. There are many kinds, you know. Mental as well as physical. He will die before you return to tell him that your mother Mina was saved."

An inarticulate cry burst from Quincy's lips.

"Oh, yes. She died during the day and during that half century when I lay true-dead.

"It was not hard to escape your father. There is no one yet who has been able to harm me! But I will do him the honor of saying that he came the nearest in five hundred years to killing me. He forgot, however, that the trail to the castle goes not only up but down. It is very hilly.

"I could hear the sound of hard-ridden horses coming after us. There were shots and the gypsies were yelling. We climbed a hill and went down into the valley on the other side. There was a crash as the coffin was thrown to the ground. For long moments, the nails held, but at last the lid was ripped open. I could see your father standing on the hill above me with the raised knife. But my eyes were not for him. I looked once more to the sky to see if the sun had set. Oh, a fraction of a second meant life to me. If the sun set before he was able to kill me, I would live.

"Your father forgot one thing, only one: he was above me, and so the sun set for me one instant before it did for him. It was so short, but it was in time. I willed myself into dust just as the blade slashed downward. I smiled to realize that I had won."

The same triumphant smile was on his lips. Then he shrugged.

"And so, for fifty years I had to sleep. I stayed as dust until that day, not so long ago, when I awoke. I was sorry to have missed so much... But then, I have seen so much."

Tony rose and stood glaring at the Count.

"Marise never has left me! You stole her with your black arts. I never thought I would come to believe in the Devil and his helpers here on Earth, but nothing is impossible now. She loved me. She never would have gone to you had she been herself."

"You are right, for once, my young friend. Had you received her dying kiss, you too would have become her helper when you died, but that other young woman screamed..."

"Yes, thank God."

"But still she was mine. Can you deny —" he moved closer to Anthony and fixed him with his glaring eyes — "can you deny that she was fascinated by me? Who made you come to the castle each night? Who but Marise."

"No, no. She hated you!"

"She loves me now."

"I don't believe it."

"You shall see!"

He stepped to the window and opened it. In a moment a bat whirled by. He spoke. Marise stepped into the room, dressed in a long black cape. She glanced at Tony as if she had never seen him before. She turned to the man who stood at her side. He slowly put his arms around her and kissed her. As she smiled up at him, he turned to Tony and said,

"You see?"

"Risa," called Tony. "Risa, you loved me, didn't you? Darling, say that you did!"

She looked from one man to another for a moment and then she spoke in the voice that Tony had heard the night she died.

"Once I loved you. But now —" Again she turned to the Count.

Like the tintinnabulation of glass wind chimes she laughed. Together they laughed, and, as the two men watched, the fog seemed to trail out the window, leaving them alone.

Tony shook his head like a man who has received a heavy blow. "I'm going to the castle," he muttered, and started for the door.

Quincy was there before him. "No, old man. Not now, not at night. We must plan. This, this creature is as wily as he is strong. We will need our brains and the help of God if we are to defeat him and save Risa."

He turned and reached into his traveling bag. "Here, take one of these. You will need it to sleep tonight. Tomorrow is the day of the battle."

Tony took the sleeping capsule in his hand and confessed, "I only want to be out of this, to be with her. I cannot believe that Risa — no. That THING isn't my Marise. Whatever she is, I still love her, God help me."

Quin laid his hand on Tony's arm in silent sympathy.

"Drink this," he said, "and sleep."

CHAPTER TWENTY-TWO

ANTHONY MORROW'S DIARY Continued

I feel as a soldier must who waits for the signal to go "over the top." A half an hour ago the innkeeper woke me, brought me a mug of hot cafe-au-lait and a note from Quin.

Tony:

(I read) Ask our host, if you can without alarming him, to find us some shovels, crow bars and a heavy hammer. Tell him some cock-and-bull story — an archeological find, mountaineering — anything. I don't wish last night's story to get out. I'm afraid of panic among the people here. An unplanned attack on the castle might ruin all our planning. I am after other weapons. I have had to take one man into our confidence, and I feel that we now have the heaviest artillery on our side. I will explain when I return.

Quin

I know Quin is right: I should dress, eat, prepare. But I can only sit and stare into the steaming cup and wonder if I am awake or in the maze of a fantastic dream.

Risa came back to me last night.

As I am a sane man, I write the truth. I don't know when Quin's drug took hold. I know I lay sleepless, wretched, utterly sickened with myself and my life. No living man had ever plumbed the depths of humiliation that I touched last night. I was thrown helpless before physical strength that defeated me; rejected by my only love. The first I could have endured. I know no human being could stand against that devil's power. But Risa's mocking laughter opened the door to hell for me.

I lay, staring into the night, trying to plan, trying to hold on to hope, for I knew that only by action could I find the strength to go on living. In spite of myself, my thoughts kept going back to a year ago, even to the first weeks here at the inn, the happy evenings with Kay and Bob, the candlelit suppers, the nights. In an agony of loneliness, I reached out into the darkness, reached for her hand as I so often had — and I felt her hand slip into mine!

My head was turned away from her. The only light was the glow of the fire still flickering on the hearth and dancing on the walls and ceiling beams. At the end of these beams were rude carvings of angel heads with blind, staring eyes and wings sprouting ridiculously from behind their ears. A sudden flicker of the fire seemed to illumine them, and the eyes turned wide and watchful, holding mine. I don't know why I didn't turn to look at her. I could feel the bed move as she sat down next to me.

"Tony, Tony. Look at me. It's Risa."

At her first word I snatched my hand from hers and shut my eyes. That voice! I recalled what Quincy's father had told us of such a voice: "diabolically sweet." It was cold and ringing like frozen crystal shattering. That wasn't Risa. It was the hideous nosferatu who spoke to me in the darkness. I knew if I looked her in the face I would be lost.

Her lips were on my shoulder, her fingers like cobwebs against my cheek. Little soft kisses traced the line of my neck, the point of the jaw.

"Remember, Tony, remember Paris? The little room under the roof, the sleigh bed and the moonlight? Tony, how could you forget me? I had to say what I did this evening. You know he made me do it. But you know you still love me. Please, love, look at me. Don't you recall our walks along the Seine and how you'd kiss me in the shadows of the bridges? Remember the night at the opera, how, when we came home Manon was ringing in our heads?"

Her fingers slid back in mine and she quoted:

"'Isn't my voice still a caress?

Just as in other days.

Isn't it my hand, that your fingers press?

Oh, take me back in your arms.'

Am I not...Marise?"

I don't think I answered her, but my mind was repeating, "No, No!"

I pushed her from me and grasped the head of the bed like a man stretched on the rack. With every ounce of will and nerve I fought her as surely as my namesake fought in the desert. But everything in me that made me a man cried out to her.

The insidious voice went on, whispering of secrets that only we two could know. I yearned for her in every way that I had loved her, and at last I knew I could fight no more. Exulting in defeat, I turned to her and took her in my arms.

The fire had nearly died and her face was a luminous shadow above me, the last flames lit an answering flicker in her eyes. I knew I loved her more than my immortal soul, and I had to be with her, even into the Pit.

I don't know what I said to her. I could feel her close to me and I hated the darkness that hid her from me. With one arm around her I reached for the night light that stood by my bed. Fumbling, I scratched a match and tried to kindle the wick. I managed to get it burning, but as I turned to her, my arm brushed against this journal which shares my tumultuous thoughts. The book fell between us, and the little palm cross that Anton's mother had given me fell from its pages. Risa's nail raked my cheek as she sprang from the bed with the open-mouthed hiss of an angry cat. Her eyes blazed like a cornered wild thing's. Her body drew back from me, arched like a bow. Her head wove sideways as does a serpent's, seeking a place to strike.

Still uncomprehending, I picked up the bit of palm, and it was as though a veil had been torn from before my eyes. That viperous monstrosity at the foot of the bed wasn't Risa. It might speak with Risa's memory, plead with a body that resembled Risa's, but the spirit I had loved was dead. In a dreadful possession, her body was made to move and speak like a puppet, manipulated by a fiend incarnated in another corpse.

Before I could act, she twirled, made for the doorway farthest away from me and my potent weapon. As if the night had not yet held enough horror for me, Risa, or the body that bore her name, slipped dematerialized through the solid locked door! This alone would have sent anyone not already numb with experience tottering to the edge of insanity.

Alone, I collapsed on the bed, spent and breathless as a man who has fought his way ashore through pounding surf. I was drenched with sweat and unutterably weary. I would not have believed it possible, but I slept.

Now, in the calm light of morning, I am drained of all emotion except resolve. I will tell Quin I am ready as soon as he returns. I shall finish my coffee and go and see the innkeeper. I do not think I'll have to invent a story for him. We both share this dreadful personal knowledge of what lies sleeping up at the castle.

Dawn was breaking over the country. Softly the world began to glow under the promise of light. Up at the castle where the sun had not penetrated for centuries, Dracula and Marise stood talking.

"It is nearly dawn," she said with a sigh.

"The last that we shall know for half a century," he answered.

He lifted her in his arms and held her for a moment before he laid her in the coffin beside the heavily carved sarcophagus.

"Good-bye," she whispered as she kissed him.

"Oh, no, beloved, just good night!"

His eyes still upon hers, he lowered the coffin lid. For awhile he stood with his head bowed and his arms folded under the long dark cape he wore. Then with a gesture of resolution, he turned and passed through the chapel door.

With the eyes of a tactician, he studied the spiral stairs and the rubble-strewn corridor that led to the crypt. Leaning against the wall was an ancient spear, propped there by some careless guardsman whose bones had been one with his native soil for hundreds of years. The Count grasped it and broke off the rusted spearhead as easily as a child snaps the head off a daisy. Using the staff as a lever, he pried at the heavy masonry of the steps. Large semi-finished stones fell loose from the shattered mortar. The stairs became more and more perilous. At last a huge section of masonry fell away, leaving a gaping hole which made the flight of stairs impassable.

Bracing himself against the still solid wall, the Count laid his hands upon a great block of stone and pushed. The cords in his neck stood out like ropes, and the strength of ten men throbbed through his iron arms and arching back. Then reluctantly, the stone moved. One final effort and the huge stone crashed against the iron-studded door of the crypt. Other stones and broken bits of masonry followed.

As a general surveys his camouflage, Dracula's gaze swept about him and he nodded with grim satisfaction. Now it was morning and if the feeble light could have reached into the corridor, one might have seen a wisp of vapor disappearing into the crannies of the rocks resting against the chapel door. It, too, was gone, and the silence took over.

Quincy Harker's notes:

Now that we are here, directly on the battleground and the last attack is about to begin, I am keeping my promise to my father to jot down events as they occur. I know Tony is keeping a record, and I know his wife left him her diary and it describes the terrible experience she endured.

I do not know how much longer I can depend on Tony. His courage and heart are strong, but I fear that he is on the verge of a physical collapse. We must act swiftly and get out of this poisonous country.

I have been up and out since dawn, and now I'll call Tony and take off for the castle.

Later

Dusk again, and another day of defeat.

Tony and I investigated every rod of that malevolent ruin today. We were not able to locate the crypt. We went down every possible passage, down every moldering staircase. Some led to storage rooms, some led to empty cellars. One even hangs broken above a rubble-filled corridor leading to nowhere.

I have reread my father's journal where it tells about the descent into the crypt, and Tony has given me Marise's diary to read. Her description of the spot is the same as my father's. How could that fiend, like some evil genie, have caused the whole chapel to have vanished from the face of the earth?

I have given Tony another soporific, and I hope he is asleep. He seems to have turned into an old man in the last twenty-four hours. I don't think he spoke more than a score of words today. Even when he was sitting quietly at the table, I noticed that his hands trembled. As he left tonight, he put into my hands his own journal for the last few days and asked me to read it. I shall take a look before I turn in.

Quincy Harker's notes, continued

Poor Tony! If ever a man has been through hell on earth, it is he. No wonder he is nearly at the end of his rope. I can hear him tossing about in the next room. I shall try to sleep now, too, for tomorrow we shall try to find the hidden crypt again.

Quincy Harker's Notes
The next day

Again, defeat. We cannot find it. I am ready to ask for help from the Devil himself!

Later

Oh, my prophetic soul!

After our supper, as we sat defeatedly in the twilight, the innkeeper approached, followed by one of the gypsies who camp near the castle. Unwillingly, the gypsy said, "There is one who would speak with you."

For a moment I admit that panic gripped me. Could it be that I was again to confront our Archenemy? But the host was translating:

"She is waiting for you at the edge of the village."

With a few words to Tony, I followed the gypsy into the dusk. I fingered the crucifix in my pocket, for I had learned from my father's journal how to protect myself against the powers of darkness which I felt I had somehow invoked.

I couldn't communicate with my guide, but I marked the way through the quiet streets. At the outskirts of town, I saw an old-fashioned closed carriage, pulled by one of the gypsy nags. As I drew near, the door opened and I could make out a dim figure inside.

A lady, a gray lady, swathed in black, beckoned me. I sensed evil as tangible as the blackness in that pale face, and I thought of Risa's words, "the malevolent gaze of an ocelot."

"You wished to see me, Madame?"

"I have heard," the voice was low with an enchanting accent, "that you are seeking the burial crypt of the Draculas."

"How did you know that?"

"This is a small village. All that you do is known here. I am, shall we say, of that family. I demand to know why this trespass?"

"That is between Count Dracula and me," I answered.

"You are his enemy?"

"I shall destroy him," I answered.

"And her?"

"And her."

There was silence. At last her voice came from far-off.

"There is a staircase that leads down from behind the dais..."

"It is shattered. The hall below is filled with rubble."

"One cannot descend?"

"One would need a rope or a ladder."

"And the hall below?"

"Almost impassable. There is a huge pile of stonework against the east wall."

"Ha!" It was almost a snarl.

I waited.

"She was very beautiful, your friend's wife."

That was not what I had expected.

"I never saw her," I said.

"I have." Suddenly her words rang clear and vindictively. "The burial crypt of the Draculas lies behind that pile of masonry. There is a chantry chapel on the east side of that corridor. You will find them there, both of them."

Before I could recover my wits to thank her, she spoke sharply to the gypsy who had been standing at the horse's head, and, with a sudden snort, the animal shot off into the night.

I returned to the inn and for the first time in days, hope grew in my heart.

ANTHONY MORROW'S DIARY
The next morning

This is the last day I shall go with Quincy to the castle. Every day I have steeled myself for the confrontation and horror of what we shall have to do, and then — nothing. This fruitless searching for that which I dread to find yet must find is more than I can bear. If I could have struck one blow and died, to finish that filthy thing that came to me in Risa's form, I think I could have died happily. But now as the days go by, my twentieth-century mind rejects the Dark Ages and my experience as a nightmare is forgotten in the light of morning.

I suppose I shall be letting Quincy down. I hear him on the stairs now, but as I'm a man and his friend, I must tell him frankly that I feel it is time to cut our losses and admit defeat.

Later

I was correct in my judgment that this must be our final day. I didn't expect Quin to accept my decision as readily as he did. I understood better when he said,

"Yes, Tony. This will be our last trip. I cannot tell you now, nor can I quite tell myself how I found out, but the riddle is solved. I obtained this in the village —" he opened a burlap bag which he had with him, "these sticks of dynamite."

"What in God's name do you intend to do, Quin? Bring that bat-infested ruin down about our ears?"

He shook his head. "It will stand. I'm only going to clear away some rubbish. Tony, I can promise you, by this time tomorrow, Dracula will be dust at last!"

"And Risa?"

He didn't answer me, but his eyes held mine with sadness.

"And Risa?" I repeated.

He dropped beside me on the bench and put his hand on my knee.

"Tony, face it. There is only one way to stop her, to give her peace."

"Do you really think I could...?"

"I will do it."

"Do you think I can let you drive a stake into her, to cut off her head, to fill her mouth with garlic, to —" nausea filled my throat and I had to stop.

"There is a better way. I told you I had to take one man into my confidence. The other night I went down to the village and talked to Father Adelbert at St. Stefan's."

"And he excoriated you for being a superstitious fool."

"No. Father Adelbert is an experienced fighter in this battle against the powers of darkness. He was born and raised here in Transylvania. His arsenal is wider than ours. There is this —"

He must have sensed my revulsion for he said,

"Look at it, Tony. It's a small, sharp spike made of silver. It isn't much bigger than a surgeon's knife. It isn't mutilating. With the priest's help, it's been prepared. It lay on the church altar pointing East during the Mass. Every atom in this spike has been magnetized for good. It is blessed, it is potent. It has the power of any sacred element, but it is more than that. It is an instrument."

At last I had to admit, "I suppose it's Risa's only chance for peace. But, Quin, I couldn't do it. I couldn't even do it with that spike."

"You won't have to. But I need your help to get into the burial crypt. Tony, come with me this one last time. Even then I won't use this spike unless you ask me to. If you aren't convinced after — I mean, if we get into that crypt and find what my father and Dr. Van Helsing found, and if you still refuse, you may take this spike back to Father Adelbert yourself. She was your wife. I must leave her fate in your hands."

I looked long at that slim sliver of silver lying on Quincy's palm.

"I'll go. I have to know," I admitted.

Quincy Harker's Notes

What a different spirit bore us off to the castle this morning. For the first time I felt free to drive our little rented roadster right up to the outer bastions of the castle. Tony and I unloaded our equipment, openly carried it through the great hall, under the minstrel's gallery, back of the lord's dais to the opening of the spiral staircase that led downward into the bowels of the castle.

By mid-morning we had retraced our steps to the end of the broken staircase. A sandwich wrapper and some cigarette stubs bore mute evidence at the stop where we had lunched, defeated, only a few days before. Using some rusty yet solid iron rings in the wall (originally, I imagine, torchieres), we secured the rope ladder and swung out over the darkness below. In a few moments I called from below:

"It isn't bad, Tony. You only have a short drop into the corridor. I'll steady the ladder for you."

Perhaps Tony felt that I was treating him like an invalid or an ancient, but he wordlessly followed me down to the corridor below. It was an arched tunnel, the roof supported at intervals by twisted Byzantine columns, each different as far as the eye could pierce the murk. I should have said, the hall was impassable, but I noticed a large gray rat peering at us with red eyes from a hole in the rubble. I shied a piece of stone at him, and he dove back into his shelter. We could hear him scrabbling away into the distance.

I stripped to the waist, handed Tony a shovel and attacked the larger stones myself with a heavy sledge. The percussion was indescribably loud in that subterranean corridor. The sound itself sent small showers of stone down from the ruined staircase. As fast as I piled up the broken rock, Tony shoveled a pathway for us. It was like excavating a road through a mountain.

Because of the dark, the noise and the choking dust of centuries, one couldn't work for too long without rest. Every blow of the sledge brought more loose stone and rubble avalanching down to impede us. In a matter of minutes we were drenched with sweat and bruised by rock falls. We worked, like Sisyphus, in a haze of fatigue that made every blow and shovelful an act of will, and then, beyond will, merely a habit of aching muscles acting without direction.

Sometime in that day we must have eaten and rested briefly and then gone on. Tony noticed that I stopped every so often to consult the wristwatch I had in my trouser pocket. Too tired to be civil, he asked, "Going somewhere, or are you planning to catch a train?"

"The sun sets at five fifty tonight. We have less than one hour left to kill the fiend."

That knowledge was like a spur to a tired horse; we set to work with vigor. Suddenly, my hammer met no resistance, and we knew at last that we had broken through the rubble into the corridor.

We scrambled into the opening and shone the electric torch down the tunnel. The columns spiraled away into the distance, balancing the heavy groined roof on their slender points. Rock and mortar crunched loudly under our feet as we made our way along the winding corridor, and the echo sounded as if an invisible army marched behind us. Man that I am, I think I would have shrieked aloud if anyone had laid a hand upon my arm.

"Grim," said Tony.

"Oh, quite," I agreed, glad of modern times monosyllabic syntax, but my mind quoted,

"Or if I live, is it not very like,

The horrible conceit of death and night,

Together with the terror of the place...

As in a vault, an ancient receptacle,
Where, for these many hundred years, the bones
Of all my buried ancestors are pack'd...
Oh, if I wake, shall I not be distraught,
Environed with all these hideous fears?"

"What are you muttering?" Tony demanded.

"Oh...Elizabethan poetry."

"What? Not your prayers?" His laughter was real, not hysteria. It was just what I needed to steady my own nerves. It startled another creature of this underworld, however, and there was a scrabble near the ceiling. Tony flashed the light upward, revealing a carving on the wall, above a monstrous boulder.

"Look, shoot it up there again," I asked. "No, higher, there above that huge rock..."

"You mean those birds?"

"Birds? Yes, but I think they are doves. See, isn't that — yes, it must be."

I hunted frantically in my pockets for a small compass. My usually good sense of direction was confounded by the twisting corridor. The swinging compass needle fluttered to rest. "Look, Tony, north. Then east is here. It must be."

"You mean the entrance of the crypt is behind that rock? It can't be. It was only a few days ago — but I"

"Remember? The Count boasted he could defeat us by both brains and brawn? I'm beginning to think there's nothing that that fiend couldn't manage."

Tony's face was ashen in the light of the electric torch. "Then he succeeded. We can never move that huge boulder in time."

"Not without help. I think the moment has come for this." I opened the sack and took out the charge of blasting powder.

I expected Tony to protest, but he silently helped me lay the fuse and wedge the caps as far under the great boulder as possible. We retreated back up the corridor, huddled against the wall, and lit the fuse.

The explosion crashed on our covered ears like the salvo of mighty guns, and the whole castle rocked and shuddered. Again, rocks showered about us, one landing within inches of our unprotected heads. Finally, the detonations ceased and we saw, with the settling of the acrid cloud, a passage cleared to a doorway. The Gothic arch of the portal and the carvings told their story. My information had been right, and the way to the tomb lay clear. It took our combined strengths to move the door enough for us to squeeze through.

On the other side, the murky daylight still held, and we could see the biers and catafalques before us. Through the dust motes dancing in the air we could make out three empty caskets, lying with their lids cast aside, and only a handful of moldy dust in their bottoms. In each one lay a sharpened wooden stake and I knew with a thrill of recognition that these must have been the tombs that were cleaned by the good Dr. Van Helsing in my father's day. I noticed, too, the horrid odor of corruption that he spoke of in the lairs of the Count. It was cloying, narcotic.

It was with great effort that Tony and I forced ourselves to move toward the great high tomb at the center of the chapel. It was piled with rock and heavy beams, as was the smaller, lighter, modern casket beside it. I knew this was Tony's moment of crucifixion. His hands were trembling as he helped me move the stones and debris away from the top of the smaller casket. Together we heaved at the great beam that lay across the two coffins.

There was no sound except our heavy breathing and the steady sifting of sand and small rocks that still fell from the shock of the explosion. With a final mighty effort we managed to shift the heavy beam and it rocked backward, out of control, and crashed into the center column of the chapel. A great crack snaked its way across the pointed dome of the room. More rock, bits of plaster and flakes from the painted ceiling settled about us.

Heedless, we cleared the top of the coffin and stepped back. Tony grasped the handles and lifted the lid. His eyes were dark holes in his blanched face as he looked, and then, his gaze misted and a strange somnolence overtook him. He dropped to his knees and his expression held the look of one who gazes in fascination at the face of one long loved. I moved beside him, and for the first time, I looked into the face of Marise, his wife.

Exquisitely fashioned of ebony and ivory, she lay in beauty such as I had never before seen. She was strangely exciting, hauntingly familiar. The face was one I couldn't have known... yet couldn't have forgotten. No wonder that even the diabolic Count had fallen under the spell of her voluptuous beauty. If only those eyes would open for me, if those red lips could glow under mine, I, too, would count the centuries too few...

Like a bolt from heaven, suddenly the main column of the crypt snapped, and a huge section of the roof crashed down upon us. When my senses cleared, I saw Tony lying face down on the ruin of his wife's coffin. Nothing was left of it. Only one pale hand could be seen under the stones and shattered wood.

I tried to revive Tony, but a large darkening lump on his forehead told me it was fruitless. The shadows were lengthening and I dared not take time for even a glance at my watch. Over my head, ominous rumblings seem to amplify. The great tomb, with the single arrogant inscription, DRACULA, was still piled high with stones and rubble. I could see the light redden beyond the clerestory windows — sunset.

In an agony of indecision I turned from Tony to the tomb, to the shattered remains of Risa's resting place. Another portion of the arched ceiling crashed down. I could hear scuttling of many small feet as the other denizens of the castle departed. There was whir of wings as bats beat against the windows, sending more plaster and rubble upon me.

Tony groaned and tried feebly to rise, but collapsed again.

Was ever a man caught in such a dilemma? Did my duty lie with the living or the dead?

I was better off than Van Helsing. The Count himself had told me that my mother was safe... and that for fifty years... if I could only seal the tomb....

My fingers touched the silver spike that Father Adelbert had given me. Would it do? I didn't know. But I had no other choice. I scrambled forward and placed it on Dracula's tomb. Snatching up two shards of wood from Risa's coffin, I made a rude cross that I put beside the silver spike, and then made another cross and laid it atop the shattered remains of Risa's casket that hid her from my sight.

I strapped the electric torch to my arm, and with Tony over my back fireman-style, I managed to get back through the door and down the corridor.

At the foot of the ladder I found my coat, and opening the flask of brandy that I had left in the pocket, forced a bit through Tony's pale lips. In a few moments his eyes opened and I could see he was dazed and only partially conscious.

To this day I don't know how we managed the rope ladder, but we struggled into the open, fresh air just as twilight fell. I no sooner got the poor chap into the roadster that he lost consciousness again. My one idea was to get Tony back to the village and get help for him.

It wasn't until the next day when Tony lay weak and bandaged in his bed in the inn that I had to make my last hard decision: what to tell him.

"What happened, Quin? Did you... is she?"

"It's all right," I promised him. "The monster's tomb is sealed forever. And Risa... is at rest."

Tony smiled and closed his eyes.

With a tired sigh, he repeated, "The tombs are sealed. She is at rest."

He slept.

But in my heart, a dreadful question lay unanswered.

THE END

www.ingramcontent.com/pod-product-compliance
Lightning Source LLC
Chambersburg PA
CBHW080958020726
47505CB00009B/2254